The Eyes &
the Impossible

The Eyes &
the Impossible

Dave Eggers

ILLUSTRATIONS OF JOHANNES BY

Shawn Harris

Alfred A. Knopf
New York

THIS IS A BORZOI BOOK PUBLISHED BY ALFRED A. KNOPF

This is a work of fiction. Names, characters, places, and incidents either are the product of the author's imagination or are used fictitiously. Any resemblance to actual persons, living or dead, events, or locales is entirely coincidental.

Text copyright © 2023 by Dave Eggers
Illustrations copyright © 2023 by Shawn Harris

All rights reserved. Published in the United States by Alfred A. Knopf, an imprint of Random House Children's Books, a division of Penguin Random House LLC, New York. Published simultaneously by McSweeney's, San Francisco, in 2023.

Knopf, Borzoi Books, and the colophon are registered trademarks of Penguin Random House LLC.

Illustration credits are located on page 253.

Visit us on the Web! rhcbooks.com

Educators and librarians, for a variety of teaching tools, visit us at RHTeachersLibrarians.com

Library of Congress Cataloging-in-Publication Data is available upon request.
ISBN 978-1-5247-6420-3 (trade) — ISBN 978-1-5247-6421-0 (lib. bdg.) —
ISBN 978-1-5247-6422-7 (ebook)

The text of this book is set in 13.5-point Garamond 3.
Interior illustrations by Shawn Harris
McSweeney's edition cover design by Shawn Harris
Interior design by Justin Carder

PRINTED IN THE UNITED STATES
10 9 8 7 6 5 4 3 2
First Random House Children's Books Edition

To all my teachers

&

to my stalwart friends
Amanda, Amy, Andrew, Shawn, & Taylor

This is a work of fiction. No places are real places. No animals are real animals. And, most crucially, no animals symbolize people. It is a tendency of the human species to see themselves in everything, to assume all living things, animals in particular, are simply corollaries to humans, but in this book, that is not the case. Here, the dogs are dogs, the birds are birds, goats are goats, the Bison Bison.

ONE

I turn I turn I turn before I lie to sleep and I rise before the Sun. I sleep inside and sleep outside and have slept in the hollow of a thousand-year-old tree. When I sleep I need warmth I need quiet I need freedom from sound. When I sleep I dream of mothers and clouds—clouds are messengers of God—and I dream of pupusas for I love pupusas and eat them with gusto.

I am a dog called Johannes and I have seen you. I have seen you in this park, my home. If you have come to this park, my vast green and windblown park by the sea, I have seen you. I have seen everyone who has been here, the walkers and runners and bikers and horse-riders and the Bison-seekers and the picnickers and the archers in their cloaks. When you have come here you have come to my home, where I am the Eyes.

I have seen all of you here. The big and small and tall and odorous. The travelers and tourists and locals and roller-skating

humans and those who play their brass under the mossy bridge and the jitterbug people who dance over that other bridge, and bearded humans who try to send flying discs into cages but usually fail. I see all in this park because I am the Eyes and have been entrusted with seeing and reporting all. Ask the turtles about me. Ask the squirrels. Don't ask the ducks. The ducks know nothing.

I run like a rocket. I run like a laser. You have never seen speed like mine. When I run I pull at the earth and make it turn. Have you seen me? You have not seen me. Not possible. You are mistaken. No one has seen me running because when I run human eyes are blind to me. I run like light. Have you seen the movement of light? Have you?

You have not seen the movement of light. But still I like you. You did not expect this or deserve this but I do. I like you.

I was born here. It's a story. My mother was housekept and still is. But when she was pregnant, she came here, to a hollow in a tree and waited for us to be born. I don't know and she doesn't know why she chose to have us in the woods rather than in the safety of her human home—for she lived then in a human home, and she has a tag and is fed daily and petted always and cared for by human doctors who have kept her alive so long, so much lon-

ger than she would have lived out here. Why she had us out here, I don't know, but she did, and when we all came out of her, oily and whimpering, she did an unexpected thing: she picked one of us, and brought that one—Leonard, my brother—to her human lair, and apparently her humans were thrilled to have her back home and delighted with her new son. The rest of us she left in the hollow of that tree.

I am not bitter.

I am a comet.

I have vague recollections of another dog feeding us pups in those early days. I have cloudy memories of that dog's smell. But was it a dog? Or was it a fox or raccoon? Janie says it was an owl. Joanie says it was a squirrel. Those are my sisters, Joanie and Janie. There is also my brother Steven. Someone fed us for those crucial first days, and it was only a few weeks before we could fend for ourselves and we did. We fended and we grew and we were good. Leonard was being fed from a kibble bag while we scrounged for what we could find in the park.

We were hungry but we were free. I still fend and I still scrounge and am still free, have always been free. No one feeds me. I am unkept and free. This is my life. God is the Sun. Clouds are her messengers. Rain is only rain.

This park is enormous. I am not a math expert but I believe it is ten thousand miles along its length and about three thousand along its width. It is long and narrow and it leads from the gray city all the way to a rough gray patch of angry ocean that meets a vast windy beach where people drown three or four times a year in the sinewy muscles of the savage sea.

I have been to this beach and have not drowned. I have crossed roads and highways and I remain unharmed. I have bitten a leg or two when necessary and I have leapt from a rooftop and came away fine.

I am strong.

I stared straight into a solar eclipse and nothing happened.

I cannot be defeated.

Maybe I'll never die.

In those early days, Joanie and Janie and Steven and I found the garbage near the snack vendors and we ate heartily from said garbage. It was so easy and we ate well. We ate half-eaten hot dogs and parts of pretzels and drank incomplete juices and sodas and spit out the sodas for they were offensive to us then and still are now. There was so much food here, so much that it was, and still is, so easy to eat often and well.

Then Joanie and Janie and Steven disappeared and it was strange how it happened. We were still puppies, I know that now. We were all puppies and were watching the humans dancing near the bridge one day, just the four of us sitting and watching the band and the dancing, when suddenly human hands lifted them, Joanie and Steven, saying things about how they were puppies and so small and so fuzzy, and I thought, *No*. I thought *No*, and told Janie *Run*, but she thought *Yes* and said *Yes*, and stayed, and she was lifted up too.

So they were taken by humans and I assume they became kept dogs—pets—and I ran into the woods where I remained free and became the Eyes.

TWO

How I became the Eyes, yes. It is a story. One day, as I ran like light through the park, I heard a rumbling voice.

"Stop," it said.

I would never think of stopping for anyone for I am free and fast but this voice was both commanding and kind, a motherly sort of voice, so I did not stop, no—I did not stop just like that, how could I?—but I slowed to the speed of sound.

"Come here please," the voice said, and I slowed to the speed of an airplane and came closer to the voice, which seemed to be coming from a fur-covered boulder. The boulder was speaking to me through the woods.

"Come closer," the voice asked, and I slowed to regular mortal mammal at top speed and came closer and saw that the boulder was a living thing, a Bison. I had seen the Bison from far away, from the road that cuts through the park and along which I sometimes run

because I like to race the cars. Oh lord I am so much faster. It's just a cruel joke how much faster I am. It is embarrassing to cars and the humans that drive them and the humans that make them. I render them silly but I am not sorry.

"Come here and talk to me," the voice said, and when I did so, I could see this Bison up close and could see that she was very old. This was Freya. I am not a scientist of time but I estimate she was six thousand years old. She is now older still.

She was one of three Bison—the other two are Meredith and Samuel—who live in a large fenced-in park within the park. They have been here always and they are slow-moving and often tired, it seems, but they have ruled the park for millions of years or more.

"I have seen you run," Freya said to me, her eyes huge and heavy-lidded. "You are very fast," she said, and I nodded seriously, pridefully. "We, the rulers of this park, need to know what happens within it, and most of the rabbits are gone now, and the owls are unreliable."

"They make up things and they have their own agenda," Meredith said, not unkindly. Meredith was the warmest of the three, the first to believe, the first to encourage.

"And of course the ducks are morons," Samuel said. He was the most cynical, the most tired, the most funny.

I knew the rabbits had disappeared, but did not know this about the owls, about their unreliability. I made a mental note

to remember that owls have their own agenda. The ducks, though—I already knew they were morons.

"We would like you to be our eyes," Freya said.

"You would be good," Meredith said.

I wanted to be their eyes. So I became the Eyes.

"Don't screw it up," Samuel said.

And so it was. My task was simple but crucial. I would run the park daily as I already did, but now, after sunset each day, I would report to the Bison what I had seen. Was there anything new, the Bison wanted to know. Was there anything troubling? Was there anything that they needed to know about that might upset the Equilibrium?

The park has an Equilibrium, as all natural places do, and the Bison watch it and protect it. They are the Keepers of the Equilibrium. If the Equilibrium is upset there are problems. If the Parks People cut a new path across the width of the park, that means more people will come where the animals had been alone and undisturbed, and that might upset the balance. If there are new buildings, that upsets the Equilibrium. New roads, new rules. All affect the Equilibrium.

The system, our system, is a good one. I see something, I tell the Bison, they conjure a solution. When there was a new road

cutting through the forest where most of the raccoons lived, I told the Bison and they decided where and when the raccoons needed to relocate. When the foxes and the squirrels have disagreements over territory, I report this to the Bison, and they decide who gets what. When a mass of humans is being too destructive and disrespectful of the land, I tell the Bison and they direct Bertrand and his birds to drop truly uncomfortable amounts of feces on these humans. Problem solved. And it all starts with what I see. The news I gather.

Most of my news is about the humans. They run and roller-skate and picnic and generally do what they should do in parks. They play croquet. They climb trees. Bikes are ridden and paths are walked. Such people are not a problem. But then there are people who are a problem. There are the Concerteers and the Campers, both of whom can be problems. The Concerteers come once a year, and when they do they play deafening music in the grass in the oval and this is a problem. The Concerteers come from near and far and generally have not been to our park before and they have no idea where they are, or that it is a place in and of itself, a place inhabited by thousands of permanent residents like myself, and not simply a stage for their standing and nodding and twirling. The Concerteers nearly ruin the park once a year with their noise and garbage and vomit and indiscriminate urination.

But they leave. They leave and we can recover.

The Campers are complicated. Some stay and have stayed for years and we know them by name and some of them are not at all a problem. Marianne and Dennis sleep in a tidy tent near the duck pond and have been here as long as I have. Thomas, near-blind, feeds birds and squirrels and lives by the sea; he's been here for what some say is a thousand years. All of these Campers are like us—they live quietly, and they walk gently, gently, gently in the woods. They respect the Equilibrium.

But then there are Trouble Travelers. These humans are not so good. They eat and drink smelly things and are sick and loud. They fight and they steal. They leave bottles and papers and feces. They attack strangers and mistreat animals. They make the woods perilous and they make them smell. Usually they travel through the park in big and loud vehicles. They are passing through, on their way from and to other places. They do not care about our home.

Most humans, though, pass through and are fine. I know this is their park as much as it is mine. The Bison understand this, the turtles and squirrels understand this. The ducks understand nothing, but that's another thing entirely.

Most humans live in their pale concrete homes on their gray asphalt streets and come through for an hour or two and I watch them. I watch the runners and horse-riders and the archers. I watch

the soccer players and soccer watchers. I watch the families and their children suddenly let loose. I watch the dog-walkers and laugh at the kept dogs. Ha ha hoooooo!

I laugh like this: Ha ha hoooooo!

Ha ha hoooooo! Pets!

These kept dogs on their leashes, they pretend I am laughing with them and not at them and that makes me laugh harder.

Ha ha hoooooo!

Ha ha hoooooo!

Delightful. Delightful. Delightful.

I laugh at how they are kept and how they pretend to be free like me. They act all casual with me, like the leash is no problem, like they would just as soon be free like me, like they could be free if they wanted, but that is a joke I laugh at with great fervor. Ha ha hoooooo! I laugh so much I cry and cry and cry enormous tears of limitless mirth.

Not-free is not free. These kept dogs know the difference and have chosen the kibble in a bag. They have chosen the under-table leftovers. They have chosen the roof overhead and the leash. The leash! The leash! The leash!

Ha ha hoooooo! I say, for I am a different breed.

THREE

I want to tell you when my days changed. It was not long ago. I would estimate it to be about two hundred years ago. It came after a night of a billion stars—siblings to our Sun.

I live in the hollow of a million-year-old tree that died a thousand years ago but still stands in the middle of the park, wrapped in ivy. So this day, after the night of so many sun-siblings, I woke in my hollow before dawn and stretched and shook. I ran like light to the ocean to wash off and to wake my-self in the bone-splitting cold of the frothy shore. On the windy sand I saw a few jogging people and some mindless jellyfish, clear and round and glistening, who had beached themselves, and saw the waking sky going from black to blue to violet to pink to orange to yellow, and then I went back to the park, clean and awake.

There was nothing happening this day. I crossed the highway like a colossus and passed the sleeping windmill and then went about my rounds. I passed the ducks' lake, which smells very bad, and there were the ducks, as usual, who do not mind the smell because they are ducks.

I crossed over to check out what the human archers were doing. There were only a few so early. One was wearing a heavy yellow cloak that tickled the grass as she walked. It looked so dramatic, this sweep of yellow against the dewy green of the archery field. Next to the archery grass there is the soccer complex and that was full of young players and their parents. I stayed to watch for a bit but strangely they played no soccer. They ran in place and jumped and sat and turned themselves in strange positions and did much cavorting and chanting and I grew weary and left.

Under a tent two humans sat at a table, and seemed to be taking money from parents and putting it into a small silver box. The money they were using was the dirty green paper I have seen; this kind I'm not interested in. I like the coins.

The coins! I love the silver, the copper. When they shine in the Sun I want them. I stare and stare. A few times I have brought coins into my hollow, but in the dark of my hollow they shine no more, so now I leave them in the Sun. Yes, I look for them to shine in the Sun so I can stare and stare.

But not too long!

You cannot stare too long or you will be caught. I will be caught. This is how Steven and Janie and Joanie were caught, by standing and staring, and I will not be caught.

Instead I look and revel in the silver and copper and then I move. I move like a crack of thunder.

In the equestrian circle, the people sat atop the horses like kings and queens as the horses trotted inconsequentially in little circles and I got bored with that, too. I went to the shallow pond where the people sail their tiny boats and there, a round man I hadn't seen before had brought a new toy boat that went very fast. It was small, smaller than me—the size of a large squirrel—and its speed was intriguing to me. The boat was low and shaped like an arrowhead and I watched it circle the shallow pond in no time.

I felt very sure that I needed to race this boat.

I couldn't race the boat if there were many humans around, but the lake was empty except for the round man and his pointy boat, so I began my rocket-running and found that I was far faster than this so-called fast boat.

I made it look like a funny joke of a boat.

I made it look like driftwood.

But then it sped up.

Aha! I thought. The boat had been holding back.

So I ran faster, and the boat sped up, and it was me against the round man and his boat, and we went twice around the pond, neck and neck. I passed the man and heard him say Whooo! And I smiled and kept running, knowing I have a different speed reserved for such nonsense, and that is the light speed I can do, which I then did, and yes I became light itself and yes I obliterated that boat and lost the man, too, in the white heat of my own immeasurable propulsion.

That happened that day, yes, but it was not the pivotal event I was talking about earlier. I will get to that.

"Are you coming or what?" a voice said. The voice was above me, so I figured it was Bertrand, a gull and my closest friend. It was time to meet the Assistant Eyes in the top of the Great Round Rock.

I did not mention the Assistant Eyes. I should have. They are my helpers. They help me see what I cannot see. We are comrades, allies. We meet each day when the Sun is straight above us, in a large rock in the park, a rock so round and high that it cannot be climbed by humans, for there is nowhere to grab onto with opposable thumbs.

On top of the rock there is a concavity, like a bowl, and that's where we meet. When we are there we have a commanding view of the park, but because of its unusual shape, no one below—no

one anywhere, no one but birds above—can see us. I can make my way up quickly, like a feather lifted by wind, because my speed is like flight and my claws like promises kept.

When I got there Bertrand was already perched, scratching his armpit with his beak, which is something he does. I don't ask why. Bertrand is a seagull, a large one. I believe he is the grandest and strongest of all the gulls, but he is humble and has never accepted this designation—strongest, grandest. He wants only to be Bertrand.

"Hi hi," he said. This is how he greets everyone. It sounds silly and delicate even, given his deep voice and barrel chest and enormous wings.

"Ho ho," I said, which is something I say back to Bertrand. It is our thing.

I asked him what was new and he said nothing much was new but that Rose-Marie, one of the gulls of his clan, had done her final flight the day before. This was not unexpected, for she was old and could not fly well anymore, and when you are a gull who is old and cannot fly, that is that. It is a cultural thing among them that I won't go into here, but when it is their time, they go out in a way they consider spectacular. I knew Rose-Marie had been good to Bertrand, and I offered my condolences.

"She taught me how to fish," he said, looking out to the sea.

"She gave me a fish once, too," I said. It has been rare in my life to eat raw fish from the sea but occasionally a gull will share, if only to see what a dog like me thinks of raw fish. Silver and flapping, eyes desperate—this was how this fish was given to me. It was a wretched experience I will not duplicate.

"She'll be missed," Bertrand said of Rose-Marie.

Of all the mammals and birds I know, it's Bertrand who is most inclined to say serious things while looking at the sea, and we allow it, we value this gravitas. He is often sought for guidance.

Sonja arrived. Sonja is a squirrel. She has a habit of showing up without saying hello, as if she's barged in on a private meeting. She's been one of the Assistants, coming to meet us on our rock, for probably six hundred years, so we cannot understand this, the way she persists with this initial shyness. She is missing an eye, and the easy answer would be that this missing eye, lost in a fight with a crow, has caused her reticence. But I'm not sure. The obvious reasons are so often wrong.

"Hi hi," Bertrand said.

"Very high," she said. This is what she always says when Bertrand says "hi hi." This is their thing.

Seeing that we were still missing two members of the Assistant Eyes, Sonja raised her small face to the Sun, something she does up here on those rare sunny days. Sonja lives much of the

time under the trees, in the shade of the pines and eucalyptus, so when she comes up here she aims her face to the Sun and in this way listens to God. With her good eye closed she looks so peaceful. When her one eye is open, the other a cinched star of fur and tissue, she looks conflicted, tense, unsure.

Yolanda landed with her usual chaos-clatter of wings and feet. Yolanda is a pelican, and a clumsy one, which is saying something, given all pelicans are clumsy, ungainly, unlikely in their shape and ludicrous in their flight.

"Hi hi," Bertrand said.

"Low low," Yolanda said. This is what she says when Bertrand says "hi hi." It is their thing. She, like all pelicans, prefers to fly low low over the water, inches above the surface, so this is a bit of an in-joke between her and Bertrand, they being creatures that fly. Yolanda also happens to be the only one among us who can read human written language, a gift she wears lightly.

Yolanda flapped her wings a bit and shook her neck, ridding herself of a bit of ocean water and a few stray feathers, and then settled down. "Where's Angus?" she asked.

Angus is a raccoon, and raccoons are nocturnal, so Angus is usually late to our meetings and sometimes does not show up at all. I have repeatedly told him that he doesn't have to attend, and doesn't have to be an Assistant Eye, given his sleep habits, but he insists that he wants to be with us, wants to be an Assistant Eye, and

I'm happy he insists. He sees much at night that we cannot. He is also a bit chubby, as are all the raccoons in this park, given the abundance and variety of food available here, so at this particular meeting, when we heard a desperate clawing at the edge of the rounded rock, we knew it was Angus pulling his rotundness up to us.

"Hi hi," Bertrand said.

"Hey Bertrand," Angus said, utterly out of breath. So far he has refused to have a special inside-joke greeting with Bertrand. "Hey everyone," he said, and collapsed. "Let me catch my breath. Go on without me."

We did, and I began by asking everyone for a general update. Yolanda said she'd seen Parks People doing some measuring and marking in the woods out near the biking oval. "Could be a new trail," she said. We all knew this measuring was close to where Angus and the other raccoons lived, but where no humans knew the raccoons lived. As far as the humans knew there were no raccoons at all in this park.

Ha, we thought. Ha ha hoooooo! There are *so many raccoons*.

I worried about the raccoons, and where they would go if the humans built a new building where the raccoons secretly lived.

Bertrand said he'd seen some new Trouble Travelers. "About six of them," he said. "They look mischievous." We agreed to keep a lookout for them.

"Have we all seen the latest in the plaza?" Yolanda asked.

The plaza, in the middle of the park, was the most human-dominated part of the park, and had been under construction for some time. For as long as anyone could remember there was a museum there, a big stone building where they kept bones and butterflies and even a great white crocodile who the birds had seen through the high windows; they claimed he was alive but no one had ever seen him move. But now a new, second building was being constructed across the plaza from the museum, and none of us could figure out what it would be.

"So far, a lot of cement," Bertrand said. "All I see every day is more cement. They bring it in those conical trucks that beep when they go backward."

For a time everyone complained together about the trucks that beeped when they went backward, and finally Angus, who had been out of breath, sat up.

"I saw something new there today, too," he said. "More people than usual. They were walking slowly around the oval in the middle of the plaza, and looking at rectangles full of nonsense."

It sounded to everyone like a typically inane and inexplicable thing humans do, so we moved on. We told stories about ducks—so many stories, all ridiculous and impossible to make funnier—and we worried together about the Bison, who were getting older and would never be free, and then we left the top of the rock and went on our respective ways.

* * *

It was late in the day, not yet night, when I realized it was Sunday. Sunday is when the people close off some of the roads inside the park so they can bike and roller-skate and walk without cars, and I have to say these Sundays are a mix of the good and the troubling. The cars I don't miss, but the number of people in the park doubles or triples and every new person is a potential hassle, and hassles they do come. On these days I have to watch for the helpers who want to know whose dog I am. The helpers who want to pet me. The helpers who want to check if I have tags. The helpers who think I need their help.

This Sunday was warm and sunny and full of humans. They laid down their blankets and ate their food on the wide lawns. They took out their cameras and took pictures of themselves in front of trees and flowers and next to other humans. These things are not so interesting but on Sundays some intriguing things happen. Near the white-glass cathedral of flowers there are people making music with golden horns while other people dance. They bring some boxes and the music comes from the boxes and they dance in pairs all over the road near the cathedral and that is something to see. They are mostly ridiculous but some are elegant and all are happy and so I watch from a safe distance and I love them all very much.

31

Dogs do not dance. I am okay with it.

On Sundays not far from the dancers there is something better even, and that is the roller-skating people. They are my favorite of all the humans. They are so beautiful. On Sundays on a side street they set up an oval and in the oval someone sets a black box onto the pavement, and from it comes music, thumpy music with horns punching above the thumping, and then the skaters go around and around the oval and they make dance moves to the music and that is easy but they are on skates—skates!—which makes all of the dancing loose-limbed and strange and sublime. From the woods I watch and watch this kind of roller-skate dancing and am brimming with bliss.

Among the skate-dancers is a man I call the Cape, for he wears one. He wears pants but no shirt and he is surely an older man of the human species but still he rules the roller-skate oval and perhaps that is why he wears the cape. The Cape goes around the oval, and he makes snaky movements, and watery movements, and sometimes he skates very low and sometimes he raises his face and arms high in the air and sometimes he rests, standing and heaving and watching from the middle of the oval as the other humans, women and men and children, go around and around.

Normally this would be all that might happen in a day, and I would report all this not-news to the Bison, and that would be that, but while I was watching the Cape I saw, using my

extraordinary vision, something new in the plaza. It was the something Angus had mentioned, but it was more intriguing than he'd implied. Beguiling even. I ran like rain to the scene.

FOUR

I normally avoid the plaza. The plaza is a gigantic tiled area in the middle of the park made for humans to walk around on, and thus there are too many humans there and too many humans in uniforms, and humans in uniforms—Parks People, Police People—are best avoided by free dogs like myself, so I don't get too close to such places. But this day I was wandering near the white-glass cathedral of flowers and then saw some new colors and shapes in the plaza, so I ventured forth but was also on high alert for the uniformed people and the helping people and all the hassles inherent in highly concentrated humanity.

Just as Angus had said, there were new rectangles, not like the maps and signs all over the park. These were rectangular, like normal signs, and they were colored, but they were different from signs. Some seemed to be pictures of rocks and boulders, but of a size that was clearly far too big and simply not right. Some were

pictures of streams that were far too wide and long and also the wrong color completely. To me this was confusing. I got closer.

I will be unhumble here and tell you that I am not a dumb dog. I pick up on things. I ascertain things. Sometimes I down-right *deduce* things. This is why I am the Eyes and why I report to the Bison and why the animals of the park generally take what I say to be reasonable and true. So in this case I inferred—another thing I do—that this was a kind of show where humans who cre-ate pictures put them up to have people walk slowly by them.

I don't know why the walking-by is important, but it was done very steadily and carefully so I deduced that the point of the whole thing was for the humans who made the pictures to have them showing on little walls, and then hope that other humans walked slowly by. The walking-by-slowly was not much stranger than the roller-skating, though I must admit it was not as entertaining.

But the rectangles I found riveting. Some showed sailboats, and I had seen sailboats in the ocean, but the humans had put the sailboats inside these rectangles and that was a pretty good trick. Some contained people, and I had seen people, too, but they had put them inside these rectangles and that was a pretty good trick, too. Some rectangles were of buildings, some were even of parks and trees, and all of them were good tricks and I felt proud of the humans for making these rectangles, given they are so

incompetent at so many things, such as running at light speed as I do with such ease and flair.

Then I saw one that was even more impressive than the others. It was about the size of a garbage can but seemed to contain another world. There was something like a human child's face but it was like a human child's face in a hurricane. The sky around the child was dark and slashy. But the child's eyes were serene! Serene in this hurricane! And there were birds all around, but they were flying upside down. And there were a thousand stars, sibling-suns, but they were somehow inside the child's body. I know how improbable and wrong this sounds, but it was all there in the picture, and there were so many more things, too. It had all kinds of objects I'd seen in the world but in a way that was impossible but seemed both scary and right and even comforting when inside that rectangle.

I couldn't look away. I was sitting on my hind legs at the edge of the forest, about twenty feet from the picture, and found myself in a state of hypnosis. If the point of the pictures was to have people walk slowly by them, this one was very successful. People walked very slowly by, and they said things to each other. One family walked past, and the father covered the eyes of his youngest child and walked by quickly, though the mother lingered for a second longer. Then, finally, the family walked away, and I stayed, looking more at the picture, luxuriating in it. No one could see

me, because with my dappled coloring I tend to blend into the woods enough that no one takes notice of me unless they are looking for dogs generally or me specifically.

That's why it was surprising when I felt a hand on my hide. I jumped, startled, and when I landed and turned, I saw the terrified face of a small human child. It was the same child whose eyes had been covered by his father just moments before. But the child's eyes were open now, staring at me for a moment before they clenched, his mouth twisted, and he began to cry. His father emerged, and asked him what was wrong. The child, in an act of treachery, pointed to me.

"That dog bite you?" the father asked, and to his credit the boy shook his head. Had he said I'd bitten him, the Parks People would be relentless in their search for me. Instead the boy made a few motions, as if he were splashing in the water.

"He's just a stray," the father said. Now another man, older—the grandfather, I assumed—approached, shooing me like I was some common animal. I figured it was time to go. I don't know why I stayed even that long. When your body tells you to go, it is imperative that you go.

I ran, was gone from the scene in seconds, but I was confused about myself. I hadn't been touched by a human in a thousand years. What was happening to me? How had I let that happen?

FIVE

In the Bison pen, I told them about the building under construction, and about the new rectangles full of gorgeous commotion. I did not tell them about being touched by a human boy, and the people shooing me.

"You say there were giant rocks?" Freya asked. "And streams a thousand times bigger than they should be? And even some human children inside a rectangle?"

"Not real human children," I said. "A picture of a human child. Like the picture on your fence." On the fence enclosing them, facing the humans, there has always been a picture of a Bison. It's a simple picture, a silhouette. I see it every day. It is just a picture of Freya and the rest of them. It is exact, it looks just like them—their size and shape. But the picture I saw of the children in the rectangle was different—it was not exact. It was

more than exact. It was like the world in a storm, real but over-turned, real but exploded.

"There was a storm, too?" Meredith asked. "Inside the rectangle?"

"Not a real storm," I said. I didn't know how to describe it. "It was just the feeling of a storm."

"And the stars were inside the child?" Samuel asked, and turned to Freya. "I think this dog has eaten one too many pupusas."

I didn't have answers. Somehow I hoped the Bison would know more than they did. Despite their limited mobility, their judgments are sound. They tell us when to worry and not worry, when to fight and when to wait. But often I forget that the Bison have not left their enclosure for hundreds of years. They were inside this fence when I was born. As long as I've lived, they have never left. Of the outside world all they know is what I tell them, what the Assistant Eyes tell me, and what they can see from the road that runs along their pen.

"I'm going back tomorrow," I told them. "And I'll get a better look. I'll be able to describe it better."

They asked me if I'd seen anything else of interest that day, and I told them only that the building going up near the rectangles was proceeding at a quick pace.

Meredith sighed. "The buildings bring more people."

"More cars," Samuel said.

"It seems to me," Freya said, "that you should be increasingly careful near these rectangles. They cause me some concern. And your great interest in them causes me concern, too. I wouldn't want you to be taken in by some kind of dark magic, some kind of seizing light. Remember the deer."

There were deer in the park, but not too many. They were not good near the cars. In fact, they were strangely susceptible, oddly vulnerable, especially at night. There were few cars in the park at night, but with their bright lights—blinding moving moon-lights—they were visible a million miles away, and so easy to avoid. The deer, though, they were drawn to the lights, and caught by the lights, and killed by the lights. Every few months we found a deer in the road, struck dead, and it would baffle us all. Why did they get so close, when the lights and sounds and smells of the cars were so obvious?

"We all have weaknesses," Freya noted.

"I don't," Samuel said.

"We all have something that blinds us to threats," Freya continued, ignoring him.

I thought of the stories I'd heard about the Bison's ancestors. Perhaps these were rumors, but I have heard that there were once so many Bison they covered the land so thickly you could barely

see the grass underneath them. But then men came, and shot them, and shot them with ease, with the Bison failing to fight or even to run, until almost all were gone. Only these three were left.

I said nothing to them about this. I have never brought up stories of their past, their ancestors' lives. There's nothing happy about those times, nothing tolerable even.

"I'll be careful," I said.

"Please be," Freya said.

That night I thought of the rectangles I'd seen, the madness within. My mind was so excitable, so scattered and bursting, that it took me a long time to find sleep. I had to do what I always do when my mind will not rest: I recite what I know to be true.

God is the Sun.

Clouds are her messengers.

Rain is only rain.

Until finally I was pulled under by the great soft hand of sleep.

SIX

The next day I went back.

I went back to the rectangles, yes. It was part of my route, first of all. Of course it was. Of course it was. It was on the way. I had to check on the building they were building, being the Eyes and all, but I also thought, if the rectangles were still there, I would briefly check on them, too.

So I ran like light, through the surrounding woods, and was sure I was not seen. I could not be seen by any human eye for I was faster than ever that day. In fact I passed a pair of starlings in the lower boughs of a live oak and they said, "You are so fast!"

And I said, "You are so good at recognizing the obvious!"

Ha ha hooooo!

I said this but they did not hear me, for with every word I had traveled a thousand miles at indescribable speed. So the words,

as I said them, were only distant memories to them, dust from planets long gone.

And I went past the cathedral of flowers, and past the roller-skaters, past the Cape, who was dancing on wheels, and then, as I neared the new building and the rectangles, I slowed down, because my favorite rectangle was still there, and I slowed more, and soon I stopped, seized by it.

It took me in. The swirl of it. The illogic of it. Why was there a child in those winds? Why were there stars in a daylight sky? And then I noticed the trees in the picture were golden, every part of them golden, as if they'd swallowed the Sun. Why? Who would have them this way, when in life they are not this way? And in the corner! In the corner of the rectangle, finally I saw a hundred or so grasping human hands, and these hands were all blue, when in life there are no blue hands that I have seen. Why would this picture be this way, I wondered. Why why why?

And then I felt the movement of air near my neck.

Then I felt a snake on my neck.

Then I heard a click.

I had been staring at the picture, wondering if maybe such a scene was possible, and would I ever see such a thing myself outside of a rectangle like this, when I felt a tickle around my neck. That was it. Just a tickle. I didn't think anything of it. I thought

it was a bug or inchworm or even duck feces—another thing about ducks—and I wanted to get closer to it, to try to understand it, and so I dropped to walking position and moved forward and then it happened. I felt a tug on my neck. I have never worn a leash but right away my mind said *leash*.

I turned around and saw the legs of a man. They were covered by green pants, and the green pants were covered in mud. I craned my head upward and saw that the man was a young man, and he had attached a leash to me. It was a simple blue rope that he'd somehow clicked onto my neck, and he held the rope in a knot around his filthy hand. I looked up at the whole of him. He was not tall, not round. He was thin, angular. He had pale pink skin and bright blue eyes and the beginnings of a yellow-red beard and wore a kind of cowboy hat with a string around his chin that held it to his angular head. His vest was black and over it he wore a long blue coat with sashes dangling to the grass. I'd seen this man before. I couldn't recall when or where but I knew he'd been identified as a Trouble Traveler. Those we never forget.

"We're gonna be a team, Splotchy," he said to me. "That's your new name, by the way." And he tugged on the leash and oh oh oh, it was horrifying. To have this rope telling me where to go. I can't explain the shock. I turned my head against it and felt a sharp pain in my neck, my shoulders. I dug my claws into the soil, to slow the turning of the planet, to stop this from

happening. "Let's *go!*" he yelled and yanked on the leash and my feet left the ground. He was stronger than he looked. He yanked, and I flew toward him and let out an involuntary yelp that filled me with shame. Then I landed and realized I was now leashed. He turned me away from the light and the pictures and into the darkness of the woods. Wherever he walked I had to follow.

I was now kept. While looking at the picture, thinking of other worlds, I'd lost my freedom in this one.

As we walked, I thought and planned. My mind was in a swirly state, though. I have swum in the gray ocean and more than twice was tossed in the cruelty of a crashing wave, rolling in the white, the shushing, the close-to-oblivion. My mind was like that now.

He walked us through the woods nearest the sea. Pulling against the leash had been painful and I didn't want that pain again unless I was sure it would come to something. I decided I needed to bide my time. Think, think, I told myself. I followed, examining the human for weaknesses. The leash was wrapped around his hand like a bandage, his bony fingers entwined with the rope and holding tight. It would not be enough to simply pull against him. He weighed more than me and the rope would not break.

After a short walk we came to a large vehicle, with great black tires and a pipe at the back spewing black smoke. The man who

held me knocked on the back of the vehicle and a door opened. "Look what I got!" he said, and again yanked the leash so my head rose to face the humans inside.

At first I saw only one of them, another man, this one with bright yellow hair and hard green eyes. But then under him, a mound stirred and sat up and became a woman with stringy black hair. Her eyes opened wide when she saw me. "I've seen that dog before!" she said. "What's his name?"

"This is Splotchy," the man who held my leash said. "I got him near the new museum. He was sitting there just looking at the art like some kind of connoisseur. He just stared and stared and so I snuck up on him. It was the easiest thing in the world."

"Hey Splotchy," the stringy-haired woman said to me. "I'm Pamela." She scratched me behind the ears, which felt so good my ankles tingled, but then other hands were touching me and the more hands touched me the more worried I got. "Twisty, you sure this isn't someone's dog?" Pamela asked.

"You see any tags?" Twisty said. "He's a stray."

Twisty gave the leash another tug, as if to show that I belonged to him. My head jerked, my neck throbbed. "I thought he'd come in handy when we make the journey south."

"We need a lot more money before we do that," the yellow-haired man said.

"We'll get it," Twisty said. "I was even thinking this little guy could help. Some family comes up to pet him, and you guys take a bag or wallet. Nice."

"Aw man," Pamela said. "That is so twisted."

"That's why we call him Twisty," the yellow-haired man said, and giggled with an incongruous falsetto.

Pamela took my snout in her hands. "Do you want to help us get some money, Splotchy? Do you want to be an accomplice?"

I wanted neither, and shook my head free.

"A few hours max, and then we go," Twisty said.

"Wait till we see what Rainbow says," Pamela said. "For now, though, get inside and close the door, dummy."

Twisty gave me a kick in the hindquarters, a yank on the leash, and I was forced to jump into the vehicle. The doors closed with a reverberating thump.

SEVEN

Yes, I had a plan to escape. Give me credit. All I had to do was get seen by one of the Assistant Eyes. Any animal at all, really, or most of them anyway—we can't count on the ducks; I've told you about the ducks—would help if they saw me leashed. Any of the other animals would know something was wrong. The task was to get noticed. But inside this vehicle it was dark, and I was far from any windows.

I had seen cars for as long as I could see, but had never been inside one. I know many of my kind enjoy being inside these moving metal boxes, but I did not enjoy it. Whatever appeal it might have held was diminished by my status as a captive. It was not pleasant. It was small and smelly and full of foul humans who wished for me a life I had not chosen.

I needed to be out in the open again, at which point I would be soon seen and soon rescued. We animals of the park have

engineered other rescues in the past. Once a month some kid traps a mouse or frog, or a Parks Person snares a fox, and we have to make a plan. With the kids it's easy—one of us startles the kid, scares them, distracts them, and their hands open and the captured goes free. The Parks People, it should be said, are generally smarter and more prepared for our disruptions.

Still, though, I knew that Bertrand or Yolanda would soon know of my captivity. They were constantly circling the park and next time I was outside, or near the windshield of this vehicle, they would see me held in the fist of this man. Or any bird would see, any squirrel. Freya would be told. The rest of them would be told. Or they would realize there was trouble when I failed to report, and they would rally the rest, and that would be that. I was of value! I was the Eyes! My absence would be noticed!

Just then, the front door of the vehicle opened, and a fourth person ducked inside, grinning with unhappy eyes. "My friends, I scored. But we gotta leave now."

"Rainbow, did you find something?" Pamela said, and crawled forward to him to kiss his cheek.

"I did, Pam-Pam," the man said. I took his name to be Rainbow, which made me laugh a little. Bearded and scarred, small-eyed and scowling, he looked quite unlike a bending prism of multi-colored light. Now his eyes fixed on me. "Where'd you get that?" he asked.

"Found him," Twisty said, and turned my leash around again in his fist. My head was brought closer to his knuckles.

"Does he bark?" Rainbow asked, staring at me.

"No," Twisty said. "He's cool."

"If he barks I'll kill him."

"He won't," Twisty said, and looked at me intensely, as if I were contemplating barking and he meant to dissuade me. "Have some of this," he said, and rummaged around till he found half a turkey sandwich. He thrust it into my snout and I resisted. I did not want his turkey sandwich, or any turkey sandwich.

"The second he barks I'll kick him in the stomach," Rainbow said. "*Then* I'll kill him."

"He won't make a sound," Twisty said, and turned the leash one more time in his white fist.

The fact is, I was contemplating barking. Barking, I hoped, would bring Bertrand, or Angus, whose ears were exceptional, even while he slept. But I didn't want to get kicked in the stomach, and I believed that was a real possibility. I had to think. I had to bide my time and use my bark at the best possible moment.

The hierarchy here was confusing. I had been sure that Twisty was the leader of this band, but now this new man called Rainbow, who was shorter but wider than Twisty, was ordering everyone around and they were fumbling and tumbling to obey.

They followed his orders without question. It looked like they'd done this kind of thing, this rapid exit, before.

"How much did you get?" Pamela asked him.

"Plenty. The park rangers, or whatever they have here, are probably looking for me, so we gotta move," Rainbow said.

"Where'd you get it?" Pamela asked, smiling with a rapturous kind of admiration.

"Never you mind," Rainbow said. He was obviously very proud of himself, so much so that his humility gave way. "Door was open, the cashbox was there, I took it and I split. Now *we* have to split."

"Out of the park," Pamela said.

"Precisely, my dear," Rainbow said, and held her face in his two hands.

EIGHT

Now I knew the shape of things. I remembered the small silver box of money from that morning in the soccer park. Soon the park police, and the city police, would be looking through the park for the culprits. They might even close down the park exits. Twisty and Rainbow and Pamela needed to leave as soon as they could. Once in the city, they would be among twenty or thirty million other people in a million cars and trucks, would blend quickly into invisibility, and I would be with them, inside this rolling metal container, utterly unseeable.

I looked around. The back of this vehicle, where I sat, was a vast boxy shape, full of random things. Two bicycles. A scooter. A horn of twisted gold, a musical instrument. And then I knew who these people were. These were robbers. These were thieves. They were truly Trouble Travelers, taking things that were not

theirs, and running away with them. There were so many things inside this vehicle. A pair of tennis rackets! Someone's purse, someone's necklace, a stroller for a child! Oh I did not like these humans.

And I knew if they got me out of the park, my chances for rescue would plummet. My friends were in the park. Only a few of the birds ventured farther. I knew I had to get free before we left the green, green park and landed on the gray, gray streets. The vehicle and all its stolen things was swiftly, loudly, rumbling through the park's main road. I could see the gray of the city in the distance in front of us.

I have to say I began to panic then. There were no openings. The windows were closed, the doors impenetrable. The only source of hope was a tiny hole in the floor, through which I could see the road rush. But it was too small, far too small for me. I would be lucky to pass a paw through it.

Never before have I panicked, because my speed is a weapon against all worry, but now, leashed and caged in this moving metal box, I could not run, had few options, was surrounded by humans with their clever hands, and I began to despair.

"I always wanted a dog," Twisty said wistfully.

He meant me. He wanted a thing, and now that thing was me. I had been a dog, a free dog of limitless propulsive capacity

and eyes without obstacle, and now I was a thing this man owned. I was the fulfillment of some desire he had.

"My parents wouldn't let me get one," he went on. "But now I got one."

"Kinda smells, though," Pamela said.

She really said this!

It is important to me that you know I do not smell. I live outdoors, yes, and partake in unwanted food, yes, and have run through mud and rain and ocean water, but I am clean. The smell was theirs! These people in this vehicle—did I tell you this already?—they smelled! Oh they smelled. I had noticed it right away, but it was more obvious to me when Pamela made this errant remark about me and my own odor. Which does not exist.

The city was growing larger in the windshield. For the first time in my life I didn't know what to do. Nothing I could do would get me free. The windows were closed. Even if I barked and leapt around and bit at random, nothing would change. And then Twisty turned me on my back and began rubbing my tummy. He did!

"Aw, I think he likes it," Pamela said.

She was incorrect.

But I was smiling.

I was smiling because, while on my back looking up, I noticed a window in the roof of the vehicle. There was a window, and

across it I saw the passing shape of a great bird. It passed quickly, but deliberately, and hope swelled in my heart.

I squirmed free and got on my feet again.

I had to be ready.

And then it happened.

A great flurry of wings on the windshield started it off. The wings were almost as wide as the glass, and blocked Rainbow's view completely.

"Gah!" he said. I don't think that is a word in any language but this is what he said. He was so surprised, so startled. He stopped the vehicle. Now the wings calmed for a second and I saw that it was Bertrand. I had assumed it was Bertrand, but now I knew for sure it was Bertrand. He peered through the windshield, looking for me. Finally his eyes found mine and he smiled a smile both confident and mischievous. I had never been so proud to have such a magnificent friend.

Thump, came another bird. Yolanda. Oh she is heavy. I had never before heard the sound of her landing on the front of a van like this, but wow it was loud. She landed, then spread her wings—so much wider than Bertrand's even!—and now there were two great birds on the hood of this vehicle, and the humans inside were screaming.

"Ahhhh!" Pamela yelled.

"Eeeahaow!" Twisty yelled.

More thumps came. More and more and more, from more and more and more birds. They were everywhere. Every window was darkened by birds, flapping their wings and cracking their beaks against the glass. Even I was unnerved, and these were my friends. Finally Bertrand gave me the briefest of winks, as if to say, *This madness is for them, my friend, not you!*

It was a frightening commotion, and was having all the desired effects: the vehicle was stopped, the humans were terrified, and soon I could be free.

But how?

The windows were still closed, the doors were closed, and the people inside seemed disinclined to open any of these openings, given the onslaught of wings and beaks outside.

Rainbow began driving again. The van lurched, and soon was moving far faster than before.

"Ha ha!" Rainbow yelled, because Bertrand and Yolanda, who had been standing on the hood and flapping their wings, were now thrust upward and behind us. They would regain their wings and catch up momentarily, but we were so close to the city, closer than ever, and once there everything would change.

And then I heard a scream like I've never heard a scream. It was so high and so loud and so spiraling I thought first of fire. Were we all on fire?

"Hey there!" said a voice, and I saw it was Sonja.

Yes! I thought. That hole in the floor! Of course. While the van had been stopped, a squirrel would have had time to make it through, and *had* in fact made it through, and this squirrel happened to be Sonja. She said hello to me as she leapt from human to human, scratching and terrifying every one of them. Oh lord she was fast! Have you ever seen a squirrel in a confined space, jumping from person to person with the express purpose of causing havoc? It is something. Never have I seen so much chaos in one small place at one time.

She was in Pamela's hair, then Twisty's, then she was all over Rainbow's head and eyes and ears until he had no choice but to stop the vehicle and throw open the door to escape.

"You coming or what?" Sonja asked me, so casually, so brightly, as if she were inviting me to look at a sunset on a Thursday.

Rainbow had fled through the open door, and was running from the vehicle, his arms flailing around his head in a way I thought very funny and very sad.

And yes, yes, yes, I followed Sonja. First I gave a nice chomp to Twisty's leg, to free his hand from my leash. Oh when that leash went slack! It was glorious, glorious! And then, with two mighty strides I was at the steering wheel, and then I leapt

through the open door, and out into the light again.

I followed Sonja back to the safety of the park, back to the woods as Bertrand and Yolanda and everyone else thumped their wings and rose above the treetops cackling and whooping in happy skyward soundings.

NINE

"Of course we saw you!" Bertrand said. "I saw you when they first put you in the van."

"From then on it was just a matter of figuring out when to rescue you," Sonja said.

We were all on the dunes by the ocean, having a bit of a celebration and recounting the rescue. Bertrand and Yolanda and Angus and Sonja were all there, as were an assortment of other birds and mammals, all telling the story over and over, laughing about Twisty and Pamela and Rainbow running around, wailing and flailing.

"Of all the rescues over the years," Yolanda said, "that was probably my favorite."

"You took your time," I said.

"You know we wouldn't have let them take you away in that van," Yolanda said.

"What I'm trying to figure out," Bertrand said, "is how that Twisty guy managed to get you on a leash. You're the fastest guy I know. On land at least."

I let that comment stand. It's a personal matter for me, whether or not I could beat a gull like Bertrand in a contest of pure speed. His velocity is aided by gravity—by falling through the sky, really—whereas I have to grab at the earth for every bit of propulsion. I decided we'd settle it another time.

"So how *did* you get caught?" Yolanda asked me, her huge head tilted inquisitively.

"Well, it was a rectangle, actually," I said, and went on to explain how I'd been staring at a strange and magical rectangle at some kind of show near the cathedral of flowers.

"Like a photo?" Yolanda asked. "Like when the humans hold the little screen up and mimic the world?"

"That's a camera," Bertrand said. "A cam-er-a." Of all of us, Bertrand knows the most about human things, and is always sure to remind us.

"No," I said, "this wasn't like anything that actually exists, I don't think. It wasn't a copy of actual life. It was like a crazy combination of actual things and made-up things and everything stuck together in this way that made no sense but seemed like the answer to a bunch of questions I'd felt in my bones."

One of the seagulls started laughing. The others joined in, cackling in their irritating way.

"Shh," Bertrand told them. "Don't act like twits." He turned to me. "I'm sorry you went through this. And we'll make sure it never happens again."

After our beach celebration, I went to see the Bison, which I had intended to do anyway. I was nervous about the encounter, given I would have to report my brief captivity, my close escape, and the embarrassing way I'd been abducted in the first place. I feared they would lose faith in me as the Eyes. They counted on me for information about the park; if I could be so easily distracted, mesmerized to the point of becoming vulnerable to being leashed, would they still see me as a reliable envoy?

"We're just glad you're safe," Freya said. "Do you want to spend the night here?"

I was touched by this gesture. The Bison were very particular about their lair, and never wanted to bring undue attention to their way of life. If I were found in their lair, for example, the Parks People would come in, inspect things and probably change things, too. They would certainly mend the hole in the fence that allowed me to enter for our nightly meetings.

"No, thanks," I said. "I'm fine."

"Maybe you need to run," Freya said.

Oh, Freya knows me!

She was so right.

I needed to run, so I said goodnight to the Bison and slipped through the hole in the fence and ran out into the park, luxuriating in my re-found freedom.

It was so good to run again. Oh-oh-oh! I had no idea how deeply the day of being leashed had affected me. I ran and ran but kept feeling a tightening around my neck. I feared that at any moment the leash would tighten and I would be yanked back to that life. Oh! You cannot imagine!

So I ran harder.

I smelled the night, I heard the trees, I named every gust of wind as I sped faster, hurtling through the park with joyous fury. Every breath I took was left miles behind me, hours behind me, oh I had never run so fast and so long! I ran through the night, circling the park, circling the park, never tiring.

I ran until I saw the first lavender light of day, and I greeted the Sun with a happy grin and wild eyes and it was only then that my muscles told me it was time. Time to stop and to rest. I found my way to my hollow and by the time I had turned and turned within and was ready to sleep, the sky was pale and sighing.

God is the Sun, I thought.

Clouds are her messengers.
Rain is only rain.
And gratefully I slept.

TEN

I woke up late, after the Sun had risen. It was the longest I'd slept in maybe nine hundred years. As I shook free of the heavy cloak of sleep, scenes of my brief captivity flashed through my mind and I shuddered with revulsion.

I had been on a leash! Just yesterday!

I ran to the nearby meadow to take in the Sun—the Sun only wants you to bask; that is truly all she wants; it pleases her to no end—and in the meadow, with my eyes to the Sun, it seemed so obvious: the Bison needed to be free.

Instantly it was so inevitable, so necessary. Freya and Samuel and Meredith should be free! They must be free. Over the years I had wondered if they wanted to be free like I was free, but because they never themselves mentioned it the notion did not much occupy my mind. But now, having been kept myself, having been leashed, controlled, held captive, and knowing the

abandon I felt as a free-again dog, I wanted the same for them. I don't know why I hadn't seen it before. Yes, my captivity with Twisty had shown me what it meant to be kept, and had woken me to the glory of liberation.

I decided I would make a plan for the Bison, and present it to them as a gift. I was happy thinking of this plan, and when I am in the midst of happy thinking I need to run, and I need to see Bertrand.

Bertrand liked all that was bold and new, and I felt sure he would embrace this particular bold and new notion. So I went to the waterfall where he liked to perch and did not find him there. I went to the garbage can, always overflowing, where he often scavenged for french fries and avocados, and did not find him there.

I hoped he would not be at his next-favorite place.

When I found him there, my heart cinched tight. He was among the archers. At the archery field, there is a long row of targets, each attached to a bale of hay. Aiming at these targets is a long row of human archers, who use simple bows and complicated bows and shoot at different times and with varying results. Some of the archers are very good, and some are not good at all.

Which makes it very dangerous and dumb to do what Bertrand likes to do, which is to fly across the field, between the archers and their targets, as fast as he can, eyes closed.

"Please don't do it," I asked him.

He was perched on a post on one side of the field. Watching. Assessing. Grinning.

"There are only six today," he said. "Almost too easy."

The field was indeed lightly populated by archers, but still, I did not understand then or ever why Bertrand, who otherwise was such a reasonable creature, would fly in harm's way like this, daring the arrows—fate itself!—to strike him down.

"But why at all?" I asked.

He looked at me seriously.

"We've talked about this," he said. "You have your running. You take pride in your speed. And in your work as the Eyes. This is like that. It's something I am good at, something that sends torrents of bliss through me."

"But when I run, there's no one shooting at me," I noted.

"Point taken," he said. "But my soul wants this."

"To fly in front of flying arrows."

"Very slow arrows, shot by aimless aimers," he said.

"I ask you again not to do it. Especially not right now. I have something to talk to you about."

"In a second," he said. "Be right back."

And he lifted himself from his perch and with three mighty thumps of his wings he was high above me, describing a wide arc that would give him the speed and trajectory he needed. I watched

my friend soar high into the white ceiling of the sky, till he briefly disappeared, and then followed his path with dread as he came barreling toward the field. He was a lightning bolt, coming at me and the field with tremendous speed. I looked to the archers, to see if they saw his approach, but none were aware. I scanned to see who among them was about to release an arrow, hoping the answer was none, but with dread I saw three with bows stretched and arrows ready.

I thought I could bark. Bark to warn them about the gull coming toward them. But that would alter Bertrand's plan, would throw into all his considerations an unplanned factor—like a sudden gust of wind. If I altered the archers' motions, or distracted Bertrand in any way, all of his calculations would be mucked up and his peril would increase.

So I made no sound.

And did not look.

I could not look.

If anything were to ever happen to Bertrand I did not want to see it. I'd decided this long ago.

I closed my eyes, and felt the rush of wind as he raced past me, and heard the release—twong, twong, twing—of one arrow, two, three. I listened grimly for the sound of an arrow's flight interrupted, of an arrow striking wing and flesh, and heard nothing but thunk, thunk, thwissle.

Two archers had hit their targets, and the third had missed, her arrow landing in the thicket beyond the hay bales.

And then Bertrand was beside me again, having flown happily back, panting and grinning on his perch on the post, very satisfied with himself.

"See that?" he asked.

"I did not," I said.

"Now what was it you wanted to talk about?" he asked.

And though I was upset with him, I told him of my plan to free the Bison, and he thought it a very fine plan, and I forgave him for his trespasses and madness, and went to the Bison to tell them of this unimprovable scheme to set them free.

ELEVEN

First I circled their enclosure, acting casually so they did not sus-
pect anything, though of course they did.

"There he is," Samuel said.

"What are you doing?" Freya asked.

"Looking for something," I said.

"Come to me," she said, and I came to her. I wove between her
legs and she nuzzled me and I did figure eights again and again
under her and I was home.

"I'm so sorry you went through what you did," she said.

I told them I was okay. I told them that in the morning I still
felt the pull of the leash, but that when the Sun burned the fog
away I felt myself liberated once more.

"You won't see those travelers again," Samuel said. "You must
forget them."

"I'm trying," I said. "It helps to make plans."

"Is that what you're doing sniffing around? I *thought* you were scheming," Freya said.

I couldn't lie to them. That had been the arrangement from the first day, when they told me I was the Eyes. I could not lie and would not lie.

"I'm planning your escape," I said.

Samuel's eyes opened wide and he smiled. "You are, eh?"

"I am. And I think I can do it. With the help of the birds and probably the raccoons we can do it. I only need some time to make the plans. I just had the idea this morning."

Freya seemed amused. "Well, I'm intrigued. And I'm grateful for your thoughtfulness."

"Would you *like* to be free?" I asked.

Samuel snorted. "How do you mean, free?"

"My son, we're not on a leash," Freya noted. "We have three entire acres to run. We come and go as we please. No one tells us what to do or when."

"I know," I said. "I just meant—"

"You have an enclosure, too," Samuel said to me. "The park. You stop when the park hits the stone human homes, do you not?"

"*I'd* like to be free," Meredith said.

Samuel gave her a hard look. "Where would you go? You're twelve thousand years old."

"I'd like to run," Meredith said.

"You never run! You can run here, and you never run," Samuel said.

"If I had enough space, I'd run," Meredith said defiantly.

Samuel snorted and Freya laughed gently.

"Meredith, I've known you all these thousands of years," Freya said, "and never have you talked about running if you had more room. This is just fascinating to hear all of a sudden."

"If I had enough room, I'd run," Meredith said again, and loped slowly off to her corner of the enclosure.

"I'll get back to you soon," I said. "When I have a plan."

"You do that, little one," Freya said, with a sly smile.

I knew she was doubtful. She didn't think I could do it. I didn't know if the Assistants would feel the same way but I suspected they would. If Freya was dubious, the others would be, too. But I knew I could do this. It was complex, yes, and had never been done before, but my freedom from Twisty and his cohorts had been achieved with heroic inter-species cooperation, and that had been relatively improvisational. If we had time, we could pull off a rescue on a larger and more impressive scale. We could free the largest creatures of all.

From then on I was determined to find a way. I had it in my head that if I could draw up a full plan, a phenomenal plan that was impossible to deny, I would convince all doubters.

The first step to convincing any of them, though, was making the plan. And it wasn't just about getting them free. The fence that kept them was not so difficult to knock down or cut, no. That could be done with relative ease. The plan had to find a way for them to get free for good. They would have to get out of the park, and quickly. And go where? The park was surrounded by corridors of gray buildings, humans everywhere till the end of time. There was only one way they could really go, and that was the beach.

I had a vision of Meredith running there. There was enough room, I was sure, for her to run and run—to gallop with abandon and to help in the turning of the planet. But the beach was full of people and was so close to the Parks People and Police People, and Meredith or any Bison would be corralled and caught in no time, yes?

They would have to go beyond the beach. In a sudden realization I knew that they would have to go to the sea, onto the sea, beyond the sea.

TWELVE

Beyond the sea? What was I thinking?

For weeks I spent all my free time in my tree-hollow, pondering, mulling, contemplating, planning. All of these tasks are tasks I am good at. Not as good as running—no!—but close. I can think. I can mull. I can contemplate and plan. Yes!

But planning an escape: this was new.

I went to Bertrand.

"We could fly them somewhere," he said.

I pointed out the weight of the Bison—that they weighed a great deal and he, and every other bird, did not weigh so much.

"But what if there were a lot of us?" he asked. "A billion of us?" Bertrand is usually so practical and wise. He really is. So this surprised me, this idea of a billion birds carrying three Bison away into the sky. I began to fear he would suggest the help of ducks.

"We could get help from the ducks," he said.

From then on I planned by myself. I needed some time to think like I run—fast and straight and right, without any mention of flying Bison.

I knew this much: that we would need to do this at night. There were four humans that worked the Bison pen during the day, cleaning and feeding and minding and generally being helpful and in the way. At night, though, there were only two, and sometimes only one—because one of the two often hid inside his car and stared at the small blue screen in his hand.

So it would be at night.

And then we'd create a distraction. Yes! When I thought of the distraction I laughed a little, because it was such a good idea that I loved my brain for thinking of it. Yes, a distraction.

That would be Angus's job. Angus would love the task, and Angus was good at it. He could tip over a garbage can, or set off a car alarm, or bite one of the human minders. Anything. We'd get that straight later.

The point was that the humans needed to be occupied, and ideally far from the pen. And when they were away, we would need one of us to open the gate. The gate was so easy to open! Or at least the humans had made it look easy with their hands, with their thumbs.

Again I thought of Angus. Angus had hands very similar in shape and dexterity, so Angus would have to open the gate, which meant we'd need someone else to do the distraction.

I thought of Sonja. She could do it. She could get a bunch of squirrels and make some noise, or break some things, or set off the car alarm and even, in a pinch, bite a human or two. All of these things were within squirrel-power so I figured distractions = squirrels = all set.

Once the humans were distracted and gone, Angus would open the gate, and then we'd move them out. Easy.

Again, from the start, I knew that it would be easy to get them out of the pen. The pen was a silly thing, such a flimsy way to contain three mighty beasts. But then, once out, what?

I would need to chart the best path to the sea. We'd avoid the wide-open spaces. We'd go through the wooded areas of the park to avoid lamplight or moonlight or roads. I started plotting the best route, and was smiling to myself, thinking of them seeing the sea. Then I wondered: had they ever seen the sea?

I honestly did not know.

THIRTEEN

"Wake up," said a voice.

I opened my eyes to Bertrand. He was standing in my hollow, which he rarely did. He had said something, once, about the smell. This comment about the smell had been hurtful to me at the time, and he got upset with himself about saying something so callous, so we never talked of my lair smell again, but he never visited again, either.

But now here he was.

"You have to see this," he said.

"See what?" I asked.

But he was already flying away. Bertrand does this thing when he wants to show me something, where he flies ahead, five or six feet off the ground, but just ahead of me. He talks and talks, so I have to keep up, and meanwhile he's leading me where he wants

to go. It's a very effective kind of moving-and-talking scheme that he has developed.

"Okay," he said, flying above and ahead and talking down to me, but not in the bad way. "I know how much you like the weird pictures in rectangles. And I know you've been wondering what's going on with that building going up near the plaza."

The building had been a mystery to us all, and this had caused some concern with the Bison. For weeks—months?—I ran by every day, checking, sniffing, ascertaining, contemplating and mulling, and every evening I would go to the Bison to report on what was happening, and every evening I knew nothing more. The building was going up fast, and there were hundreds of humans going in and out, clattering and sawing and knocking and yelling, and yet I couldn't get any more clarity on just what the building was for. This lack of clarity was causing the Bison to lose a bit of faith in me, I worried. I also knew that since my brief captivity they, and everyone, had worried about me, thinking I was traumatized, or somehow affected, or somehow less-than-I-was-before. None of which was true. I didn't think it was true. I worried it was true.

"So," Bertrand said, still flying above. "I was at the new building just now, and listen. First of all, that thing is enormous. It's like the biggest building you or I have ever seen. Definitely the biggest thing in this park, okay?"

I never knew if Bertrand needed me to say *okay* when he said "Okay?" So usually I just nodded to get him to move on and keep him telling the story.

"There aren't too many windows," he continued, "but there are some, and I was perched near the top, where they have those little windows so the Sun comes in?"

"Skylights," I said. Bertrand was so intelligent, so worldly, and knew more about the human world than all of us, but occasionally he did not know a word I expected him to know. I had introduced to him the word *pupusa*, too.

"Right. Those," he said. "And I was there, looking down inside, and man, there were like a thousand pictures in there, and some of them were even stranger than the ones you told me about. I mean, it's like they're on *every wall*. And most of them look like they were made by loons."

Loons really are strange, by the way. Ducks are irresponsible and self-centered, but the loons are just plain strange.

"And there are people inside?" I asked.

"Just a few. And they're all wearing white uniforms. They're the Picture Police—like the Park Police, but for the rectangles. They don't do the walking-by-slowly that you say the people usually do. They're not touristing. They're working."

This news about the pictures didn't make me too excited, though, because immediately I knew this wasn't the kind of

building where my kind would be welcome. Free dogs are not let into museums, or any buildings, really—not that we would want to go. Why would we? And with Picture Police walking around, the likelihood of me getting inside was dim.

Bertrand doesn't always show it, but he's very intuitive and empathetic, and he seemed to read my feelings at that moment.

"I'm telling you all this," he said, "because I was talking with some of the other Assistants, and we're going to get you into that building."

"There's no way," I said.

"There is a way," he said. "There *will* be a way. And we all know you've been feeling off lately, what with being dognapped and all. So we're going to get you into that building no matter what. You'll love it and you'll feel better completely, okay?"

This time I figured I should say *okay*, so I said "Okay."

FOURTEEN

Could Bertrand be right about this—that a building full of chaos-rectangles would soon be real? The thought of it overtook my mind. I decided he could not be correct. He must be mistaken.

But I had to prove it. So that evening I went to the building. The woods hug the back of the building, so I believed I could get close without being seen, but I will admit I was wary, so much warier than I was before. I found myself looking over my shoulder every few seconds, moving like a skink, never in a straight line, never sitting still. I had to be sure no one could sneak up on me ever again. The thought of it—of being caught by the Trouble Travelers and their rope!—continued to fill me with shame. My idea of myself had diminished. Until my captivity I thought I was faster, cleverer, closer to invincible.

As I approached the building, I followed Bertrand's instructions to the entryway. It was a pair of large doors, big enough to

drive a car through, at the bottom of a sloping driveway. When I got close enough, though still hidden in the woods, I saw no one and nothing there. The doors were closed and there was no sign of life. But I was sure this was the place Bertrand had described, so I waited. I waited and thought of pupusas, for it had been many days since I had eaten a pupusa with fervor.

Then a truck appeared. It was the size of a delivery truck, the kind that sometimes passed through the park to drop off human food at the snack bar. It stopped at the driveway, turned around, and backed down the sloping drive slowly, letting out a high-pitched sound all the way. And here I should say that of all the horrible things humans have created, the most maniacal and wrong of them all is this, this intermittent screaming sound as their vehicles go backward. All of life stops when the screaming begins. All beauty ends, all music ends, clouds cleave, hearts break, and all of the world nearby waits, with breath held, for the sound to end. Nothing can be done during this mechanical wailing. No thinking, no eating, no running, no living.

And the humans could so easily correct it, but they do nothing. Some human invented this sound, and they all know it's a terrible mistake, but they all live with it, as if it were an unchangeable part of existence, like weather or death.

Finally the truck stopped backing up and the screaming ended, too, and the world was allowed to begin again. The tension that

had overtaken my body let go, and I watched as the back of the truck met one of the building's giant doors. The truck's engine was cut and a man jumped down from the cab. He was wearing a white jumpsuit and a blue hat, looking like the ice cream man who used to drive his truck through the park (though that is no longer allowed). He walked to the back of the truck and rolled the door up. It thundered as it rose, its peak punctuated by the loudest of clacks.

Another man appeared from inside the building, and the two men talked a bit, and then went into the truck. They emerged carrying a huge rectangle, almost as long as the truck itself, and covered in plastic. There was some trouble getting the end of it out of the truck, though. Something got stuck, and they put it down, and when they did, I got a good look at it. In the rectangle I saw what seemed to be an impossibly large rock, and there was something like fire, and there were a thousand enormous trees, trees far bigger than any I'd seen, and there were many, so many, tiny humans wearing crowns. Oh, it was beautiful. It was so wrong and right!

But I had to look away. I knew I had to look away.

I could not get hypnotized again.

Could not become like the deer.

Could not become again what I'd become before—kept!

So I looked away. And when I looked away, I saw something. I saw something by the pond. The pond! The new building was next to the park's peanut-shaped pond. Did I tell you that? I should have told you that.

The pond is a man-made pond. It is a dirty pond. It is a smelly peanut-shaped pond and it is full of ducks, because if ducks love anything, it is a smelly pond.

And this particular smelly pond is one the humans love, because they can sit in plastic boats and pedal their feet and go so slow it makes me cry. They like to paddle their boats under the little bridge that spans the narrow part of their peanut-pond, and atop this bridge, this day, I saw something.

There was a little girl there, atop the arched bridge, a tiny person just getting used to walking, and she was bobbling herself across the bridge and doing so in that clumsy way very small people do, as if her legs were two pogo sticks of mismatched lengths. Like I always do, I looked around her for the parents or siblings or watcher of this child, but this time I saw no one.

The thing about this bridge is that it's not safe. The humans of this park are interesting in that they make everything very safe and tidy for other humans, especially in those places where the humans most congregate. Whenever they make a new building or bathroom or path, there are little handrails and signs to be sure

that no human falls or becomes confused. But these older places are different. I figure the pond has been here for about ten thousand years, so it is not subject to these careful planners.

And while I watched her, I began moving toward her and the bridge. My legs compelled me, my feet moved without my asking them to. I was moving through space slowly but steadily toward her, because sometimes my legs and feet have a kind of second brain, a kind of auxiliary intelligence that gets me out of trouble but in this case got me into trouble.

The paddleboat pond is one of the busiest places for humans, and this bridge is very popular, and it was always curious to me how they let it remain so rickety and so full of gaps. The bridge had a railing, and had a line of columns that held the railing to the bridge, but these columns were weirdly spread out, leaving wide gaps between the columns, which I'd always considered odd. Anyone could so easily slip through.

So my legs and feet continued to bring me closer to this girl, because something was about to happen and even before my brain or gut knew it, my legs and feet did.

This little girl on the bridge was wearing a yellow dress and white socks and was carrying a plastic doll—a tiny grown woman with long brown legs. She shook it as if trying to wake it from a deep slumber. She was paying no mind to the bridge and the gaps in the columns, and I thought, There is a decent chance this girl

will slip through one of these wide gaps and will drop into the pond below, which is about six feet deep and not at all clean.

Then again, I thought, every day I saw humans on bikes near cars speeding by and always I knew the possibility of collisions and calamities, but these imagined collisions and calamities had never happened in my presence. In all, I saw so many near-accidents that I had begun to think the park was somehow immune to misfortune.

By this point I'd reached the far end of the pond, and was watching the girl on the bridge from a safe distance, in the high grass that surrounds the pond, when I sensed—sorry, it was the smell—the presence of turtles.

First of all, I love them.

Everyone knows I love the turtles. They are cool. I am cool and they are cool, but they smell, always they smell, in large part because they swim in this peanut-pond, which smells. I told you about this smell.

"Hey," I said to the turtles, and one of the turtles, whose name is Gregory, said "Hey" to me.

So as I watched this toddler on the bridge, still alone, and still perilously close to the edge, I knew in my heart that it was another time when I was seeing what might happen but which would certainly not happen. And yet no adults or guardians of any kind seemed to be claiming this child, or seemed concerned about her in any way.

"You see this?" I asked the turtles.

"Hm," Gregory said. He turned his attention to the girl. "Where are the parents?" he asked.

And now a few other turtles stopped to watch, too, all of our heads going back and forth, looking on one side of the bridge and then the other for some sign of a human that would whisk this toddler to safety.

And then she dropped into the water.

There was no preamble or prelude.

She was standing one moment.

The next she was falling.

She fell face-first, as if she were intent on finding something at the bottom of the pond, her eyes open and her expression serene and even curious as she fell waterward. All the while, she held tight to the long-legged woman-doll. When she landed on the black water, her weight made a considerable splash, the plastic doll striking the surface with a high-pitched swack.

"Oh no," Gregory said.

On the days when I swam in the ocean and watched the humans swim in the ocean, fighting the savage waves, I was accustomed to a certain delay between the crashing water and the re-emergence of the human face, whipping the water from their eyes and hair.

So when the child hit the water, the turtles and I all gasped, but waited a split second to see if the toddler would return to the

world above the water. After the splash, though, this toddler's face did not emerge in the usual time, and so the rest of the turtles also said, "Oh no!" and for some reason unknown to me I said, "Yup," and I jumped from the shore.

I had never saved a child from drowning before. In the ocean there were only those times when you heard, the next day, about the drowned, and thus my memory only gave me thoughts of the drowned, the news of the drowned, and nothing about the saving of the drowning. I had no idea what to do, but in seconds I was upon the child, who I was grateful was now floating at the surface, but with her rear pointing upward and her head underwater.

Push her head up? I asked myself.

No, I told myself, *drag her to the edge of the pond.*

So I grabbed her rear with my teeth, holding her tightly without breaking the skin, and I swam, sideways and frantic, to the farther shore, where the people were. I needed them to see her. In flashes I saw the colors of the humans standing near the snack bar, and hoped one of them would see us, would see this dog dragging this child through the water. And finally one of them did.

"Check out the dog dragging that hairy garbage around," said a young man, and I knew we would not be so easily saved. He was a human but could not discern what was happening, what I was doing, that it was a child I was saving.

I kicked frantically, continuing onward. Soon I sensed the far shore coming. I struck it with my head but knew I couldn't get out. The sides were covered with algae. Normally, with great effort I could swim, get momentum and leap out, but not while dragging a child. I could only hope to lift my head and bark, hoping for someone to see us as real, to see this child as a human child, to reach in and pull her out.

So I let the child go and lifted my head from the water and barked as loud as I could. The child began to drift away and now I grabbed her again and pulled her to the edge of the pond. Again I lifted my head and barked. Nothing. I tried it all again, and on the third try finally I heard someone scream, "A baby! A baby in the pond!"

And from there all went quickly. Human legs ran to us and hands reached in and the child was lifted high and carried away. I was ready to swim away and disappear but someone lifted me, too. When they put me on the pavement I made it clear, by shaking the water from my fur and acting as hearty as I could, that I was not in need of help. I stood, with people all around me, some of them taking videos and pictures with their small screens, and all the while I watched as they put the child on a green park bench and tried to revive her.

The crowd was three people deep and I tried to weave inside it to see. Someone had found a doctor, and she was doing doctorly

things and it was only then, with the girl on the bench, that I saw the child's face up close. She was bluish now, and her eyes were closed, but I saw her beautiful heart-shaped face, the softness of her, and while I was taking her in, and worried for her, desperate for this to be over and her breathing to begin again, I had the feeling that I might lose my sense of my surroundings, might be hypnotized again as I had been by the picture.

So I backed away, and when I backed away I heard someone say "Hold that dog!" and the voice that said those words did not seem congratulatory toward me or grateful or anything good. This was a disciplinary sort of voice, so I ran.

At the speed of sound I was in the woods and over the main road and into the next forest, and from there I cut west toward the ocean and took the trails as far as the windmill and then went to my hollow and hunkered down there to wait out the storm, thinking my thoughts:

God is the Sun.

Clouds are her messengers.

Rain is only rain.

FIFTEEN

"I've been looking for you all night," Bertrand said. It was dark, so dark, a purple kind of dark that made you feel you were falling into it. I'd stayed hidden inside my hollow, afraid of being found, or blamed, and most of all afraid that the girl in the dress was no longer a child but was now a former child, a being no longer living. "Now I found you!"

I did not think it was so clever to find me in my actual home, but I said nothing. I was aching. I was so twisted up inside, afraid to ask about the child. I couldn't ask. I wanted to be told. I waited for Bertrand to offer the information. The seconds were endless. What about the child? I thought.

"Oh, she's fine," he said casually. "She woke up right after you left. And then everyone was looking for the hero dog, but you were gone. Why'd you leave?"

"I got scared. She was blue," I finally said.

"Well, she's fine, and they took pictures of you, so everyone knows what you did," Bertrand said.

And immediately after he said it, I knew we had a problem. Hearing my troubled silence, Bertrand realized the problem, too. If the humans knew what I looked like and what I'd done, I would no longer be able to run freely and invisibly in the park, and everyone would be looking for me, and if everyone was looking for me, I could no longer be the Eyes. I could no longer be free.

"Maybe it'll be okay," Bertrand said, though his tone said quite the opposite. His tone said it would not be okay.

SIXTEEN

On top of all this, I had caught some kind of bug. I knew, because the ducks liked it so much, that the water in that pond was unclean, but ingesting it—oh!—it was far worse to have swallowed that water. What I'd contracted I didn't know, but it gave me the sneezes and halved my energy.

I stayed in my hollow for the day and night after the rescue, and the day after that, Bertrand and I made a plan. To test the situation in the park, I would run as the Eyes, and he would follow me from above. We would see which humans were out and about and might be watching for me. We would see if I could continue to be free.

The Sun was still rising above the trees when we set out, but immediately Johnson and Sharif, two of Angus's raccoon friends, stopped us. They were out of breath.

"They're everywhere," they said.

"Who?" Bertrand asked.

"The humans," Johnson said. "There are Parks People, and Parks Police, and some kind of other police, and people with huge cameras. They're all over the place. You can't go out there."

"They had one of those Control-the-Animals trucks," Sharif said. "It was big."

Every so often, the Control-the-Animals people came to the park to take out an animal who had bitten a human, or an animal that was not where she or he was supposed to be. Yolanda was once pursued by the Control-the-Animals people when she had gone fishing in the peanut-pond. It was a lesson to us all—do not linger where you are not expected. Do not upset the humans' version of the Equilibrium.

It did not mean that the turtles couldn't leave their pond or that I couldn't converse with the Bison. It meant only that being too obvious or showy about any of these unexpected appearances would bring the Control-the-Animals people, and they were not to be trifled with. They had cages and tranquilizer guns. I'd seen even the craftiest of the raccoons taken in minutes. The gun would be pointed, the gun would go pop, the tranquilizer would do its work, and the animal would be packed up in a cage and taken away. Where to, we never knew.

"Let's just wait a day," Bertrand said. "The horses are sensing a storm later anyway."

So I stayed in my hollow.

I remained hidden and listened and looked and thought. I thought about the strangeness of salvation. I had saved the girl and now I was a hostage in my own home. If I had allowed her to sink, or had simply watched and waited for someone else to save her, I would still be free. I would be able to run untethered and she would probably be fine—saved by another. It seemed a clear truth that helping with anything or anyone at any time brought with it a unique kind of burden. Because I had always moved at the speed of light I was unseen, and the unseen are uniquely free. But being slowed, stopping altogether—there were problems with this. I had been captured when I stopped to see the rectangles, and now I was hiding because I had stopped to save the girl. Stopping was a problem. Stopping meant captivity. Helping meant captivity.

The wind outside picked up.

But then again, I thought, Bertrand and Yolanda and Sonja had helped me when I was a captive of the Trouble Travelers, and their interference returned my freedom to me. So that was an undeniable good, I thought. Maybe it's always complicated. No help is simple because no one being helped is simple. The notion that everything was complicated was itself sort of simple, and that made me smile. If we go through life assuming everything will be complicated, and then it *is* complicated, doesn't that make us

better prepared? What I mean is, if we expect life to be complicated, and life *is* complicated, then life is simple, right? I needed to tell Bertrand this thought I had, this wonderful circular idea I had. I had a feeling he'd like it.

Then the rain began. It began with dusty taps on the earth around my hollow. The dry brown dirt around me got wet and went black. I listened to the rain grow from taps to slaps to the hush of rain when it comes in teeming hordes. I decided I could wait to tell Bertrand my new idea.

Rain is only rain, I thought drowsily.

I slept on and off throughout the day and realized I was overtired. I needed rest. I needed this time alone with all this tiny water from the sky. I smelled the sweet eucalyptus on the wind, such a sweet smell when mixed with fresh rain.

SEVENTEEN

They say I slept for weeks.

It seemed like years. Centuries.

I slept through days, I woke up in sunlight and woke up in moonlight and always spiraled back to sleep.

My bones were tired. My muscles were tired. My skin, my fur, my eyes. I was tired of seeing, tired of doing.

I dreamed and dreamed but my dreams had no interpreter.

And finally, one gray day, I woke, walked outside, and saw them all. Bertrand. Yolanda. Sonja. They were all standing outside my lair, as if waiting.

"We've been waiting," Sonja said.

"A while now, since sun-up," said Yolanda.

This meant a great deal, she implied. I didn't know what I was supposed to say.

"What do you want me to say?" I said.

"You've slept enough," Bertrand said.

"No one needs that much sleep," Sonja said.

"The point is we care about you," Bertrand said. "The Bison care about you, and would like to see you. We'd all like to see you up and about and running. And seeing."

"Even the ducks," said Yolanda. Of all the people who didn't love or trust ducks, Yolanda was probably the most duck-unloving and duck-untrusting, so hearing her say this hit me hard. She cared about the ducks wanting to see me. It messed with my mind.

"The Bison want you out there," Bertrand said. "We've been picking up the slack, but not so well."

"They have been a bit snippy about it, to tell you the truth," Sonja said. "They have so many questions, and even with all of us helping, we miss things."

I began to feel better. Better because they had failed at that which I excelled. I was ashamed at my pride. Just then, the Sun broke through the cloud cover and shone on me, warming me, loving my face, and I loved the Sun back. *I love you too*, I said to the Sun, because her love was so obvious and real.

"But everyone knows what you look like," Yolanda said.

"There are photos everywhere of you," Sonja said.

"*Wild dog*, they say," Yolanda said.

"Photos and little posters and even diagrams," Bertrand added.

"So you can't go out like yourself."

I didn't understand. Maybe I'd been sleeping too long. I couldn't go out like myself?

"If you go out as yourself, they will know you as the *hero dog* who is also a *wild dog*, and you will be leashed again," Yolanda said.

"And caged and kept," Sonja added.

"Probably sent away," Bertrand said softly.

The Sun had made me calm. The Sun had made me wise. The Sun had made me understand, instantly, the truth of what they said. I could not be seen in the park the way I had previously been seen.

"So we got you this," Yolanda said. With her beak she presented me with a lump of bright pink. I had seen it, this lump, next to her this whole time. Now she—all of them!—were suggesting this pile of pink was somehow meant for me.

"What is it?" I asked. I suddenly felt suffocated, and surrounded, and this pile of pink was an affront, a smothering thing. I thought of bolting.

"It's a disguise," Yolanda said. With her beak she turned the pink pile into something recognizable—a sort of garment. It was tubular, and made of wool, with five gaps: one in the top-left; one in the top-right; one at the end, two on the bottom.

And finally it dawned on me that this was something I was supposed to wear. They saw the horror on my face.

"It's ridiculous, I know," Bertrand said. "Obviously it's terrible,

but that's the point. This is what *kept* dogs wear. What *pets* wear. You will look like a silly pet of some silly human, dressed in pink and wearing a collar. Sonja?"

Sonja now produced something far more offensive than the pink garment. It was a collar, studded with bright plastic diamonds, meant to be worn around the neck. It was an attack on all that was good and right.

"I can't wear that," I said. "That or the pink tube. No."

"Then stay in your hollow!" Sonja spat. "Just stay and sleep and never come out again!" I'd never seen Sonja so agitated. "Why do we care if you never come out again! We don't care! No one cares!"

And she turned and ran off.

Bertrand turned to the rest of the Assistants.

"Can you excuse us a moment?" he asked in that exhausted-but-wise way of his. The Assistants all flew and scurried off, settling about fifty feet away. When they were out of earshot, Bertrand turned back to me.

"We are concerned about you," he said.

"Thank you," I said evenly.

"I ask you to trust our collective wisdom," he said. "We have thought this through a great deal. And we have come to a series of related conclusions. Can I enumerate them?"

I sighed. I looked down. I looked up to the Sun. I breathed

in. I breathed out. I did not like it when Bertrand took it upon himself to enumerate things. It tightened every bolt of my being. I took a deep breath.

"Sure," I said.

"First," he said, "you need to leave your hollow and be part of the world again. Second, you cannot leave your hollow looking like yourself. That is self-evident. Third, as you know, we have begun planning a way to get you into the museum to see the hundreds of rectangles that will no doubt please you greatly."

This third item did get my attention, and Bertrand noticed. I smiled, picturing myself among the pictures inside that building. But then he looked at me with something like mischief, something like pity.

"Lastly," he said, "we have devised a brilliant disguise. We, your friends."

Because Bertrand is very smart, he knew he needed to dwell on this point, this mention of my friends, who cared about me. If they had all gotten together and thought, collectively, about my well-being, about what would be best for me, how could I flout it? What monster would turn up his snout at the thought-through help of all the friends he had?

"Okay," I said.

"Okay what?" he asked.

"Okay I'll try on the get-up," I said. My plan was to put it

on, deem it ridiculous and convince everyone else that it was ridiculous, too.

So Bertrand tossed me the pink garment and the sparkly collar, and I ducked my head into the sweater and instantly I was stuck. The opening at the neck was too narrow so I was helpless inside, in the dark of the doggie sweater.

"Help?" I asked from the darkness.

Bertrand and Yolanda tried to help, but their beaks were imperfect tools for the job. They were pulling the woolen sweater apart.

"Stop," I said. If the sweater were a mess the effect would be lost. A dog sweater, as demented and unnatural a thing as it was, must be pristine. We needed opposable thumbs.

"We need Angus," I said.

"He's sleeping," Yolanda said.

"Wake him," I said, a bit too harshly. I realized how desperate I was to run again. "He'll understand."

When Angus arrived, he was not happy. A nocturnal creature, he was halfway through his rest. I could not see him, given I was still stuck in the sweater, but I could hear his weariness in his voice.

"The thing is," he said, "everyone's always got an emergency requiring opposable thumbs, and no one thinks it can wait until nighttime. But you know what? It *can* wait. It can always wait. Now what's all this? What's that funny lump?"

"That's Johannes," Yolanda said.

"Why's he wearing a doggie sweater?"

They explained it to him, and I tried to help explain, but Angus couldn't really understand me from under all that wool.

It's important to note that while Angus, and all the other raccoons, acted annoyed to be woken up and asked for help, they took great pride in their dexterity and cunning. They liked showing off their opposable thumbs, and liked to complete any such mission in as little time as possible, as if to show how easy it was to do things that for the rest of us were impossible.

"I'll get your paws through first," Angus said, and helped me disentangle my claws. He pulled one paw through and then the other.

"The head part is funny," he said. "It's so thin, and your head is so big," he said, laughing. "I wonder what kind of dog used to wear this. It must have had a tiny noggin!"

"Can we get on with it?" I asked.

"Did you say something?" he asked. "I can't understand you under all that sweater."

The opening for my head was indeed very small. Angus had to pull on it from various sides, widening the gap.

"Try pushing through now," he said, and I tried. I made no progress.

"You must have some pit bull in you," he said. "Only pit bulls have such huge heads."

Angus had Yolanda grab one side of the sweater, and Bertrand

grabbed another side, and Angus pulled himself, and we heard a tiny ripping sound.

"Oh no!" Yolanda said.

"Don't worry. We're just stretching it," Angus said.

They continued stretching until Angus was satisfied.

"Try again now," he said, and I pushed, and with my snout I could finally feel the cool air outside. I pushed and pushed, and Angus continued to make adjustments, squeezing out one ear and then the other, until I could see again, and soon enough my head was through.

"You're in the world again!" Bertrand said, and laughed. "But didn't you have a tail before?"

Angus scrambled to the back of me and pulled my tail through the horrifying little hole meant for tails.

"That's better," he said.

It was not better. The sweater was a wretched thing. It scratched me everywhere, like I was enclosed in a thicket of dried weeds. And though I could see, this was not a plus, for now I knew that about fifteen birds and animals were gathered around me—where had *they* come from?—and many of them were fighting back their laughter. When Angus put the collar on, their barely held laughter escaped in tiny squeaks and sighs.

"Very dignified," Yolanda said, covering her mouth with her great gray wing.

This sweater was a terrible thing for me. I felt very bad, very

ashamed, very much like I wanted to be deep in my hollow, alone and in the dark. But then Bertrand did the kind of thing he was known for doing—a wise, rational, convincing and impossible-to-debate thing.

He brought over a piece of glass. The animals of the park had grown accustomed to glass. We saw it on the buildings, the cars, the windows of the homes that bordered the park. We knew we could see ourselves in the glass, and so our reflections were not foreign to us. We knew what we looked like. For instance, I knew, before this day, that I was a breathtaking paragon of muscle and speed.

And now, when Bertrand brought a piece of glass before me—he'd planned it! he'd planned it!—I knew I was a ridiculous clown-dog clad in pink and fake diamonds.

"It will work," Bertrand said.

EIGHTEEN

None of us knew what would happen. Would I actually blend into the world of humans and kept dogs? The sweater covered most of my dappled coloring, disguising me, but I was still the size and shape of the dog they were looking for.

Bertrand decided to stick to the original plan, with him flying overhead and keeping track of me and any approaching problems. If he saw vehicles or humans pursuing me in any way, he'd swoop down and let me know.

"Ready?" he asked.

"I am," I said.

He flew up and caught a thermal and floated above me like a guardian cloud. "Get going," he yelled down to me.

I began. I took the earth under me and sent it into the past. I did it again and again, taking the future and tossing it

backward, and soon my eyes were glassy with cold speed and I was flying. I broke the speed of foxes and rabbits and kept going. I entered the speed of sound and broke it like a cheap toy. When I was flying across the picnic fields and could see the windmill and could smell the salty ocean, I became light itself.

When I slowed down I realized I'd crossed the highway and was already in the oceanside sand and could feel the surf on my toes. If I hadn't stopped then I think I would have flown across the surface of the sea. I made a note to try that another time, and I smiled. I laughed. I could still run. I looked up and saw Bertrand hovering up near the Sun.

"So far so good," he said.

You are wondering about the sweater. You are wondering if the sweater altered my running ability, or my ability to reach the speed of light by throwing the future into the past and being the mechanism that turns the world.

I am here to tell you that it did not affect this ability, and I have to give credit to whatever human loons had designed and made this garment. For years I—and every free animal I knew—made glorious fun of these sweaters, and looked with pity upon the dogs who wore them.

But now that I had run in one, I knew that it did not inhibit my movement. It warmed my body, which I appreciated, especially when I got close to the sea, where the wind often cut through me

with sharp chilled fingers. In all, I was able to run just as well as before, and was warmer than ever. Not bad.

But it still looked ludicrous, and the collar was an insult to all that was dignified and right.

I ran more, and ran along the water till the beach ended at the great jagged boulder, and ran the other way, till the beach ended at the high white cliffs, and to see how fast I could move up slanted sand, I darted up the cliffs and found myself almost bumping into Bertrand. He was perched on the cliff, staring out over the sea.

"Coda," he said.

I followed his stare and found the tiny silhouette of a seagull soaring high, crossing the Sun in ever-higher ellipses.

"Who is it?" I asked.

"Louis," he said. Louis had contracted some kind of illness, something the gulls got, and soon would be unable to fly. So he was taking this final flight before he lost the ability altogether. "Look how beautiful!" Bertrand sighed.

I said nothing. I did not and do not approve of this thing they do. They consider this act—coda, they call it—full of honor and heroism and sacrifice, but I consider it self-indulgent and silly and unnecessary and grim. When a gull is getting very old, or if they have sustained an injury or illness that will prevent them from flying again, that gull decides on a time

and place for their final flight. The coda—their last time on earth. Even if they've been wounded grievously, and can barely flap their wings, they will manage one last flight. They go out to sea, and they fly high, as high as they can manage, and they circle if they can, and then, when they reach their apex, when they feel the heat of the Sun—the warming touch of God—they let go. They let go, and spiral down, and give themselves up to gravity and the water, and when they hit the surface of the sea, that is that. That is the end of them.

This is what Louis was about to do. He was flying higher, his ellipses ever-more melancholy, and Bertrand thought this was just wonderful.

"It's wonderful," he said, shaking his head. "That's the way I'll do it when I do it."

I turned away from Louis and his coda, not wanting to see the last of it, and I ran down the cliff and down the beach. Bertrand is my brother, and we know each other and agree on most things, but this coda-madness I cannot abide.

Wonderful? No. Heroic? Not a chance. There is no reason the gulls cannot go on living even after losing their ability to fly. They can walk—they walk very quickly and well—and they can find food, and can talk and see and enjoy just about everything about this singular and precious life.

But they see their loss of flight as a loss of face, a shameful thing that embarrasses not only themselves but their species. They call it dishonor, and for a million years they have done this, this terrible coda, and I cannot look and will not look. I don't approve and won't watch.

When I ran back into the park, I took another way, hoping to see the roller-skaters and the Cape, but as I got closer I saw more cars and humans than I'd ever seen before in the park. I was running just below the speed of sound, so it was hard for me to count, but I would say there were at least twelve and a half million people there, all around the new building. There was some kind of band, and there were many smells of many foods, and there were millions of children—maybe nine million?—and umbrellas of a thousand colors, and I thought I had to stop or at least slow down so I could see what this was all about.

But there was no place safe where I could sit and watch. There were no trustable woods with a view of the building's entrance. I could take my usual spot at the back door where I'd seen the giant impossible pictures enter, but that was quite removed from all of this, all of these people and excitement. I circled the building at the speed of a jet and thought about this, about how to get

a bit closer. So many of the humans present had their dogs with them, all of them on their leashes, and so many wearing those silly sweaters—

Oh! I thought. Oh! Oh! For a moment I had forgotten that I, too, was wearing a sweater. I laughed to myself about this.

Ha ha hoooooo!

With so many kept dogs and so many of them silly-sweatered, I could blend in, even though I had no leash and no keeper.

I slowed to the speed of the fastest car and got a better look at the plaza. I looked for Control-the-Animals people and found none. I looked for wary-looking Parks People and found none. The event was festive and crowded and no one, I was sure, was there looking for me. I slowed to the speed of a slower car and swung into the crowd.

"Museum's open," a voice said above me.

It was Bertrand. He was doing that thing where he flies right above me such that I can't see him. No matter where I craned my neck, he would float left or right so I couldn't see him. He thought this was the height of all worldly hilarity.

"Stop that," I said.

"Stop what?" he asked, still invisible to me.

I didn't know how he could be so playful and wry after seeing Louis's coda, but again, this particular gull-madness eluded me and I have chosen not to try to understand it.

"Go away," I said.

"Fine," he said, and floated near my shoulder. "Looks like they're opening the building. Now all the people can go in there and see those crazy rectangles you like."

I couldn't go in, I knew.

He knew, too.

"But there's a couple rectangles visible from the outside," he said. "There's a giant window and they have a few big ones, bigger than a bush, hanging in the front there. You'll see."

I went to see, and I saw.

There were two, and they looked nothing alike. They didn't look like the same species could have done them both. The one on the left was like the ones I'd seen before, in that there were things I recognized. There was a jagged boulder, though it seemed to be upside down, balancing precariously. There were a hundred or so people, and most were chartreuse. There were roads, and there was a giant chicken being ridden by a man with the head of a chicken. There were a hundred other things in the picture, and I couldn't see them all, because there were so many slow-moving people near the painting. I was not surprised by this—it was a tremendous picture—but it was annoying, too, to have it so difficult to take it all in.

The one on the right had no things in it, nothing I could place in the world. It was just colors and shapes. There were stripes,

and ovals, and I think there might have been a triangle. And then half the painting seemed to have been dipped in midnight. It was a liquid darkness that took me in and I became part of it, living inside it. I found it very confusing and mesmerizing, too, and I was staring at it—it was messing with my mind, to be honest—when I felt the flapping of wings near me. It was Bertrand. He landed near me and, for the sake of the humans nearby, he pretended to eat some popcorn on the grass.

"Move on," he said out of the corner of his mouth. "You're being noticed."

I broke the spell of the picture and looked around. Several humans were looking at me; they'd noticed me hypnotized by the picture.

"Check out the dog who likes art," one said. Another was taking photos.

"Pretend like you're waiting for your owner," Bertrand muttered out of the side of his beak.

I looked toward the front door and whined a bit, like a kept and needy dog would. A woman in a uniform, who I assumed was attached to the museum, started walking toward me.

"Time to move," Bertrand said, and flew ahead.

I trotted away from the museum, but found myself among more humans than I'd ever seen. I weaved between legs, always

watching every which way, tingling with a fear that one of them would have a leash and would leash me with it.

Finally I got clear of the throng and was in the open grass in front of the white-glass cathedral of flowers.

"There he is," a different voice said. I turned to find a Control-the-Animals person approaching me from behind, with—with—with—

A leash!

Another leash.

There was another Control-the-Animals person in front of me. They were converging on me, one with a piece of paper bearing an image of a dog. It was me!

I ran before I could think. I ran like the birth of the universe. I left the open park and entered the darkness of the woods and wove through the trees as a swallow would, as a hummingbird would, and I did not slow until I was sure there could be no one near, no one who could have followed, and finally I arrived at my hollow, where Bertrand was waiting.

"I think we have a problem," he said.

"Yes we do," I said.

"The sweater helps a little," he said, "but those rectangles still get you in such a trance that you're putting yourself in some serious danger. And I'm saying that as your friend. The way you were

looking at those rectangles was concerning. You zoned out to the point where you could have easily been leashed again. Or caught by the Control-the-Animals people. Or—"

"I know, I know," I said. I didn't know what else to say. I was embarrassed and I was concerned, too.

"But listen," Bertrand said. "We're going to get you into that building. I don't mean while humans are there. I mean sometime when it's empty and you can take it all in without attracting attention and endangering yourself."

I didn't know if this was a good idea or a horrible one, but I was intrigued. "I'm sorry to put you guys through all this," I said.

"It's nothing," Bertrand said. "What else are we supposed to do? Eat pieces of bread and french fries all day? We need some kind of higher purpose. And maybe that higher purpose is keeping you from harm, and getting you into that weird building with all the demented rectangles."

NINETEEN

For the next week Bertrand and his gull-friends did what they called *reconnaissance*. It meant they flew and hopped around the museum and then gathered outside my hollow and used their beaks to sketch their ideas to get me inside. They squabbled among each other, and flapped their wings haughtily—they did this to make their points, and their passions, known—and then they left again, to gather more information.

Meanwhile I was told to stay unseen. The rescue at the peanut-pond had brought unwanted attention, and then my staring at the pictures through the museum window, even while wearing the pink sweater, had made it worse.

"There is talk," Bertrand said, "about this unusual dog in the park. Or unusual *dogs*, plural," he added. "No one is sure whether it's one dog, or two, or a whole herd of eccentric and

sometimes-heroic dogs who sometimes wear sweaters. But there is curiosity out there. And it's best that you stay out of sight for another few days."

So I did.

I stayed in my hollow and slept. I lost track of days. I dreamed while awake and was awake while dreaming. I slept so much I thought I'd forget how to wake up. But then, two or two hundred days later, Bertrand woke me at my hollow one pink morning.

"Okay," he said. "We have a plan. We're getting you into that building."

"It's a pretty good plan," Yolanda said. I had not noticed Yolanda was there. Now I saw that everyone was there—Sonja, too, and Angus, and everyone seemed excited about this plan.

"It could work," Angus said. I was surprised to see Angus awake in the morning, and more surprised to see he had a few other raccoons with him, too—including Johnson and Sharif. They were crafty and experienced with getting in and out of places they were not meant to be.

And nocturnal as they were, they all looked shockingly awake. They were smiling with clenched teeth and unblinking eyes. I didn't want to know what they thought, but it was clear they were less optimistic than the birds. They were there out of a sense of duty, but their opinion about the plan seemed iffy.

"It's an interesting plan," Sharif added finally.

This is a thing with raccoons. They think their plans are better—always better—but then they offer no such better plans. Instead, they squint a bit, smirk a bit, as other animals explain *their* plans. And then the raccoons go along with these plans, because they have no plans of their own. It is an ongoing thing that is maddening if you think about it too much.

"The signs say the museum is open every day but Monday," Yolanda said. "So Monday's the day. One woman comes in the morning and opens the building."

"From the loading side," Bertrand added.

"We're assuming she shuts down the alarm," Yolanda said. "So once that happens, we're halfway there. All day there are cleaners and workers who come and go from that same door. It's propped open from time to time, too."

"It's very accessible," Sonja added. "Weirdly easy."

"But what about the humans?" I asked.

"That's where these guys come in," Yolanda said, and nodded to Angus and Sharif and Johnson.

Sharif and Johnson were still smiling the stiffest of smiles. Everyone stared at them, and they said nothing, as if not wanting anyone to confuse the plan with anything they would have concocted themselves.

"The doors will be open," Yolanda continued, "so it's just a matter of Bertrand and I finding the right time."

"To fly in?" I guessed.

"Indeed," Bertrand said. "We'll fly in, one at a time, though we'll immediately take different routes, both of us heading toward the top floor."

"It'll seem logical to the humans," Yolanda added, "to have the crazy birds head upward to the skylights."

"There's a room up there that has a door," Bertrand continued. "We'll fly into that room and perch up in the highest window frame. All of this is in hopes that all the humans in the building chase us, get all worked up, and spend a bunch of time trying to catch us, get us down, et cetera."

"And meanwhile I roam the museum?" I asked. Something about it jabbed at me. It wasn't quite enough. It wasn't the right higher purpose.

"In part," Bertrand said. "But Angus will also be waiting at the doorway to sound a warning if any of the humans head down in your direction. If that happens, you'll have plenty of time to either hide, or make for the exit. Same way you came in."

"And how many humans are usually there on Mondays?" I asked.

"About eight throughout the day," Yolanda said, "but no more than four at any one time. We were thinking the best time would

be midday, when there's only two there. That's between shifts, I assume."

"Once they see us all, they'll call the Control-the-Animals people," I noted.

"Of course they will," Bertrand said. "But it usually takes them a few hours to get here—to get anywhere." Bertrand then turned to me. "You think that'll be enough time?"

I didn't know what to say. I'd never been inside that building, and didn't know what was in there. "I have no idea," I said. "And I haven't agreed to this yet."

"No," Yolanda said, with compassion.

"I mean," I continued, "couldn't we all get caught? Or at least one of us?" I had a terrible premonition just then that it would not be me that got caught, but one of the birds. I pictured fragile wings mangled in a heavy net, beaks straining, terrified eyes. But the birds themselves seemed wholly unworried.

"The beauty part comes in there," Bertrand said. "When the Control-the-Animals people come, they rush up to the third floor with their nets. That's when you, Johannes, exit."

"You're first out of the building," Yolanda said.

"All of the humans head up to the third floor," Bertrand said, "because they've been told it's two birds. But right when they're on the stairwell heading up, Sharif and Johnson appear, heading down."

"They run right past them!" Yolanda said, laughing suddenly and helplessly, her eyes wet.

Bertrand was grinning. "Sharif and Johnson lead the people onto the second floor, leaving the third floor pretty much empty. That's when we get out of there. We both fly down to the loading dock and out, while everyone's chasing the raccoons."

"What about Sharif and Johnson?" I said.

All along, the raccoons continued their tense, unsettling smiles. There was no animal more clever and open to wily and even diabolical plans, but they seemed unsure about this one. At the same time, they were clearly afraid to hurt the feelings of the birds who had planned it so carefully.

"Apparently there's a garbage chute?" Sharif said dubiously.

"There is," Yolanda said. "It leads to a dumpster in the basement."

"It's been proposed that we go through the garbage chute," Johnson explained to me. "And into the dumpster."

"And how do they get out of the dumpster?" I asked. I thought I was looking out for my raccoon friends, but Sharif didn't take it that way. He looked at me like I'd asked how they know how to eat food.

"We can get out of a dumpster," he said flatly.

TWENTY

I was still keeping a low profile, so I stayed out of sight, turning my friends' plan-to-get-me-into-the-museum into my plan-to-get-the-Bison-out-of-their-enclosure. This, I knew now, was the nobler purpose Bertrand had talked about.

The planning kept my mind off my own troubles, and gave me the same sense of mission Bertrand spoke of. Every reasonable creature knows that the worst thing any creature can do all day is think of themselves. If there are troubles in your mind, you should think first of the troubles of others; it is the essence of liberation. That is, freedom begins the moment we forget ourselves.

And my purpose, I was convinced, was to liberate the Bison. The idea intoxicated me. Every moment of the day I pictured them running free, on the beach and then on plains and through forests. I was unsure where these plains and forests were, but when I saw Freya and Meredith and Samuel running, free of

fences, I smiled and felt it might be the work I was meant to do on this earth. And that they would be proud. They would be proud, would be away and running in some other place, and I would likely never see them again, but they would look back on me and feel proud of me.

It was not that I did not feel their pride in me. Freya had entrusted me with being the Eyes and had never wavered in her support of me. And yet I felt something, some creeping lack— some sense that they expected only so much of me.

But what if I did something extraordinary?

What if I liberated them and sent them into some new and transcendent level of existence?

They would think differently of me.

They would be surprised by my ingenuity. My ability to rally the animals and pull off the impossible.

So I continued to work out the wheres and hows and whos. I wondered how many raccoons we would need: as many as possible. I thought about the escape being at night: it must be. I thought about the escape being during windy, stormy weather: this would help. I thought that our best chance would be on one of our dark and moonless nights, when the winds whip and hunt. When branches crack and break, when the human lights go out, when the roads are closed by fallen trees.

That! I thought. That would be the time!

TWENTY-ONE

During this low-profile time, even though I couldn't be the Eyes myself, my reports to the Bison still needed to be made, so for the next few days I skulked to the rounded rock—going slowly, slowly, skulking so slowly it pained me, it ruined me, it was so humiliating to go so slow, but going fast would bring attention. At the rounded rock, I would scamper to the top to meet the Assistant Eyes and ask them for their reports. I would listen to these reports, determine what was important and what was not, and then Bertrand would convey my report to the Bison. It was not a perfect system but it was all we had.

This particular day, I waited at the rounded rock for the Assistant Eyes to arrive. First was Sonja, and as usual, she acted as if she had interrupted a private gathering.

"Oh, hello," she said. "I'm just here for the meeting. But I can leave if you want…"

I reminded Sonja that she'd been coming to our meetings for six hundred years, that she was a valuable member of the team, and our friend to boot, so there was no need for this shyness. I wanted to tell her that I'd said exactly this to her a million and one times, but didn't, because already she had begun to smile.

"Okay," she said. "So I guess I'm here."

Angus scampered up at that moment, which was startling, because never before had he been close to on time, and by my estimation, this time he was early.

"I got a clock," he said.

I didn't know what a clock was. I turned to Sonja, hoping she did, and that she might explain it, but her look was blank.

"It's a human thing," Angus said. "It tells you when to do things and go places. I got one, taught myself time, and now I'm always prompt. By the way," he added, "our meetings are at noon. That's the time-word for when the Sun is straight above us."

This was too much information for me to take in all at once. Angus was using a human device and would always be prompt? It seemed against the natural order of things. But then I remembered I was wearing an unsightly human-made sweater, and thought: *Hm! Seems we are all going through some significant changes!*

And I decided not to say anything more about it.

A great warm shadow swept over us and I knew Yolanda was above. She landed with her usual chaos-clatter of wings and feet.

I said hello, and Angus said hello, and Sonja just squinted through her remaining eye in a way that seemed friendly.

We waited for Bertrand on the rounded rock, and I wanted badly to begin. To get our reports out of the way, first, and then begin to plan again for the escape of the Bison.

"Anyone seen him?" I asked.

"Not for a bit," Yolanda said. "I saw him by the windmill earlier in the morning. But that was some time ago."

"Speaking of time," Angus said, and started talking again about his new clock, and I found myself losing interest, and so I looked up to the Sun bright above. The Sun appreciates it when we appreciate her, we must remember, so even as Angus droned on about the definition of time, we raised our faces to the Sun and took in her warmth.

Finally we heard a sound from above, a whistle growing louder. I looked up and it was a dot, then it was a bird, then it was Bertrand.

"Whoa boy! Whoa whoa whoa!" he yelled. This is what Bertrand said when he descended quickly. It was something he'd heard a human say once while riding a horse. He landed, and paced back and forth on the rock, his back arched and his feathers still ruffled.

"Do I have news!" he said. He was huffing loudly. "There's a bunch of weird animals near the windmill. They're unlike anything I've ever seen."

"Are they raccoons?" Angus asked.

Bertrand gave him an exasperated look. "I just said they're unlike anything I've seen. *You* are a raccoon, and I have seen *you*, so how could these be raccoons?"

"So they're not raccoons," Angus concluded. There was something in his eyes, though, that hoped—suspected even—that they really *were* raccoons.

"How many of them?" I asked.

"Hundreds!" Bertrand yelled. "Millions! They're all over the park by the windmill. We gotta go now," he said, and turned to me. "And you don't have to worry. No one will be looking at you in that sweater with this going on."

TWENTY-TWO

And so we all scampered down and made our way to the windmill. Bertrand and Yolanda flew overhead. For years the windmill
area had been covered with tulips, a gorgeous chorus of colors
that bloomed like a million tiny sunrises. But then, a short time
ago, some kind of weed had taken over the area, killing the
flowers and every other nearby plant. These were weeds with
prickles and spikes and barbed stalks. Every one of us, even the
birds, had had unfortunate experiences with these weeds and their
anti-social features. I had scars on my legs and hindquarters, and
Angus, who had tried to scamper under them, had a nasty streak
that started on his shoulder and ran all the way down his back. As
we approached the windmill, I got pre-emptively annoyed about
Bertrand bringing us all to see these stabby weeds and their floral
victims.

But then we all gathered behind some bushes, on a rise with a view of the windmill and its environs. From there we saw the hundreds, or maybe millions, of new creatures that Bertrand had promised.

"They're eating the weeds," Angus said.

Indeed they were. We watched as the animals continued to fan out. When we arrived, they were in a close formation, but as we watched, they spread like water, devouring the tough and spiky weeds like they were the most delicate desserts.

"What are those creatures?" I asked.

No one knew. They had long hair or fur, curved horns and four legs—skinny legs—and stood a bit like horses, but they were more the size of large dogs. And they were eaters. They ate and ate and ate. It was astounding the way they ate.

"I would have never thought to eat those weeds," Angus said.

"They go at them like they're dandelions," Sonja said.

"I don't understand it," Yolanda said.

These weed-devourers never paused. We watched for hours and they never stopped eating.

I didn't know what we'd be reporting to the Bison.

"Maybe tell them a hundred tiny horned horses are about to eat the windmill?" Angus said.

I knew we needed more information. For example, where had they come from? Every so often there was a new animal in

the park. We all remembered, for example, when the first loon arrived. The ducks were so happy to have a bird nuttier than themselves. But we'd never had an invasion like this: a species like no other, and in such vast numbers.

"Do we talk to them?" I asked.

"I think we do," Bertrand said.

But we couldn't just barge down to the mass of eaters and announce ourselves. The way they were eating the weeds was chilling. Would they eat us, too? They seemed like vegetarians, but how could we be sure? There were so many of them. A thousand? A million? They could disappear the five of us in seconds.

"Look," Angus said, and pointed to two of them, both a bit smaller than the others. One was black-spotted and the other was the dull color of red clay. They had wandered away from the pack and were making their way to us.

"I can get closer," Bertrand said. Bertrand was always brave and never scared, and always liked to be first in line for danger. And he didn't really think much of it. He said these things and did these things naturally, as naturally as I ate pupusas and Angus opened complicated containers. "If they go under the bough of that pine," Bertrand said, "I'll be close enough to talk to them but far enough away that they can't eat me."

We all told Bertrand to take care, and he rose into the sky, circling high before swooping low and heading to the tree in

question. Meanwhile, we all hid in a dense thicket where we could hear the ensuing conversation.

Bertrand dropped in with great elegance and settled on a bough. He looked down to the two sample creatures. "Hello friends," he said to them. He was perched above, looking friendly enough, casual even, though decidedly out of eating range if they thought him delectable.

The two animals looked up, mumbled hello with mouths full, and went back to eating. This was a start, we all thought. They spoke our language, and they chose to speak—or mumble—to Bertrand, and not to eat him.

"Welcome to our home," Bertrand said, and smiled down to them. I thought he sounded very regal and magnanimous, and I was proud of him, but the eaters didn't look up this time. They nodded almost imperceptibly and continued eating. It seemed very rude to me.

Bertrand cleared his throat. "Can I ask where you all come from?" he asked.

The two eaters looked sidelong at each other, as if imploring the other to be the one to answer the question. It was clear that neither of them wanted to stop eating. Finally the black-spotted one raised his head. He was still chewing with a rounded, incessant motion of his powerful jaws.

"We're from the main-land," he said, his mouth full. Then he went back to eating with renewed devotion.

Bertrand nodded calmly, as if he'd just been told the most logical and expected thing. But none of us had ever heard of anything called the main-land. We knew what *main* meant, and what *land* meant, but the two words together meant nothing to us. Angus looked at me and I shrugged.

"The main-land, eh?" Bertrand said. "Remind me, where's that again? You mean the gray human settlements surrounding the park?"

I was so happy Bertrand asked that, because it was precisely the question on my mind, too. I would have been too embarrassed to ask.

Again the two eaters looked at each other, begging the other to be the one to explain. Every time one of them had to speak, this meant time away from eating, and neither could abide the sacrifice. I thought I saw one of them roll his pale eyes. Finally the reddish one raised his head.

"The main-land?" he said. There was a know-it-all tone in his voice. "The main … land? The main … land?" He did not sound so polite or so respectful of Bertrand, and I found myself growing impatient with the impertinence of these two furry eaters.

Bertrand looked down at this reddish one, smiling but befuddled. "I don't understand," he said.

"You're on an *i-land*," the red one said matter-of-factly. "A *very small i-land*. When you leave here, you cross the sea and you hit the *main-land*, which is a billion times bigger than this place."

TWENTY-THREE

It's difficult to convey the effect this information had on me, on all of us. We stopped breathing.

And then a human voice emerged from the pack of weed-eaters. He made a kind of high-pitched sound, and the two animals we'd been talking to turned and abruptly left. They joined the rest of their kind, never saying *Excuse us* or *Goodbye.*

"What a strange species," Bertrand said.

Because there was a human nearby, we thought other humans might be nearby, too, so we slunk away, planning to regroup on the rounded rock. Once there, we were all individually more confused than before, and collectively more confused than that.

"They sure like to eat," Yolanda said. "Anyone notice that?"

"And what about that main-land thing?" Angus said. "Do you really believe we're on an island?"

Bertrand was silent, and I had the feeling he felt responsible—
that knowing the extent of the land we stood on was something
his perspective might be uniquely suited to.

"None of us could know," I told him.

"I should have known," he said. "All my life I've stayed close
to this park, afraid to fly over the sea, and I should have ventured
farther. I would have found out."

"But none of the birds know, do they?" I asked.

Bertrand contemplated this. "I guess not. But still…"

"Don't feel bad," Sonja said. "None of us knew."

"I should ask the Bison," I said. "I wonder if they knew all this."

"I wonder, too," Angus said. "But you can't see the Bison in
that sweater."

Everyone chimed in, pointing out that visiting the Bison
would be impossible wearing bright pink. The Bison-minders
would notice instantly.

"You want me to take it off?" I asked. My heart filled with the
glorious thought that I would soon be free of this itchy cocoon.

"It always comes down to me," Angus complained.

"It most certainly doesn't always come down to you," Bertrand
said.

"Stuff like this does," Angus said, but he was, as always, secretly
happy to show off his opposable thumbs. He began pulling at the
neck of the sweater, but as difficult and painful as it was to get the

sweater on, getting it off was far harder.

"Yelp!" I said. I did not mean to yelp; it made me appear weak, I knew. But yelp I did, for the pain was great.

"Hold still," Angus said. "Can anyone help?"

Bertrand and Yolanda attempted to help.

But when they grabbed at the sweater, they pulled its threads and it tightened around my neck. Again I cried out. They let go.

"This is useless," Angus said. "We can't get it off."

And he sat back on his haunches.

Bertrand breathed loudly through his nostrils. I knew this giving-up of Angus's would not sit well with Bertrand. Giving up was the hallmark of the impatient, of the weak, he often said. He could not countenance it.

"We'll have to take it apart," Bertrand said.

"Nooooo!" Yolanda moaned. "It's so beautiful!"

But it was the only way. Because Angus felt slighted, and because Bertrand was offended by Angus's giving-up, Bertrand turned to Sonja.

"Can you help us?" he asked.

Sonja's one eye brightened. She had small fingery claws, and she could make things, yes, but more than that, she could take things apart. She could shred anything with those tiny claws. And quickly she went to work. She pulled on the threads, she cut them, she scraped and snapped and shredded. And soon what had been a

143

sweater was just a tangle of loose thread, which I stepped from as if from a bad dream.

I smiled to my friends. "Thank you," I said.

Sonja was blushing and fidgeting and her one eye was wide open, in a kind of ecstasy. "And thank you especially, Sonja," I said, and she turned her head downward. She couldn't stand the praise.

"It was nothing," she said.

I made my way to the Bison alone. Their human minders were sometimes nearby in the evening, so I needed to be careful. There was one in particular, a man who watched from—and was usually asleep in—a hammock near the outer fence, who I had to be mindful of. He was a thin, white-haired man who wore a bright red vest for warmth. I made a wide arc around him and then traveled an unusual route, through unknown thickets and irrational paths, until I made it to their pen. I found them all lying in a huddle, on a far corner with a view of the sea.

"My son," said Freya. We nuzzled. "Stay low," she said. "The people are not far." With her head she pushed me to lie down beside her. Between the three Bison-boulders, no human could possibly see me.

"We worried for you," Meredith said.

"I'm proud of you," Freya said. "Your bravery with that

child was conveyed to us. By Bertrand. I'm so proud. But we miss you."

"Your Assistants are not good at this job," Samuel said.

"Hush," Freya said. "They'll get better. They're trying."

"They're not suited to it," Samuel said.

"Maybe Sonja," Freya said.

"Yes, Sonja is the best at the work," Meredith said. "But you were born to be the Eyes."

I was happy to be so praised, happy to be missed.

"But I can tell you have news," Freya said.

"We saw about a hundred new animals today," I said.

"A hundred different new animals, or a hundred animals, all of one kind?" Freya asked.

"Just the one kind. A hundred of them. Lots of different colors," I said. "They're new. I've never seen them before."

The Bison asked me to describe the new animals and I did— hairy and hooved, with narrow faces and rough-hewn horns.

"And you say they ate incessantly?" Meredith said with a smile.

"Sounds like goats," Samuel said.

I had never heard this word, *goat.*

"We had some here long ago," Freya said. "Maybe a thousand years ago."

"At least that long ago," Meredith said. "They did love to eat."

"Were their eyes like those of a cat, very bright, very light,

and with long narrow pupils?" Freya asked.

"Yes," I said. "Their eyes were much like a cat's. But with the pupils going left and right, not up and down."

"Yup, sounds like goats," Samuel said.

"I think, dear Samuel, that we've established they are goats," Freya said. She turned to me. "How many did you say there were?"

"About a hundred," I said, but I realized it could have been a thousand. "Or a thousand." Actually, I thought, it could be far more. "Somewhere between a hundred and ten thousand."

"And did they say where they'd come from?"

I explained the word the goats had used, *main-land*, and how they said we were currently on an *island*, and that where we lived was very small compared to this other place, the *main-land*, and how this made me feel very confused, and a bit small.

Freya's eyes had grown sad. "I'm so sorry, son," she said. "We do live on an island. I was born on the mainland." She said the word quickly, as one speedy word. "Samuel was born on the mainland, too. But now we're here, and we're happy here. Here is home. And there's no way to leave."

TWENTY-FOUR

When the goats said this, about the main-land, it was one thing. They were cat-eyed strangers who ate prickly plants without pause. But having this new knowledge confirmed by Freya was quite another thing. I sat between them, asking questions, and finally I was stunned silent. The world beyond this island, they told me, was a million times larger. We lived in a small replica of the main-land, they said, and of the rest of the world, they said. There were other main-lands, other islands, so many millions of places, they said. They said all this in whispery tones, knowing the profound effect it would have on me. To have all known boundaries removed, exploded, replaced by a universe of endless elasticity—it is not an easy thing. My mind struggled with this new concept of spatial infinity.

And just when I needed most to be with the Bison, to bask in their warmth and wisdom, Meredith saw one of their keepers.

"He's coming this way," she said.

I peeked over the shoulder of Freya and saw a human with a light—a light attached to his head—walking toward us. It was the hammock-man.

"Run," Samuel said.

I got to my feet.

"Don't run," Freya said.

"Run," Samuel said again.

"No, it'll make too much noise," Freya said. "Just slip away. Slink along the fence till you find a hole, and scurry through."

With the human-light coming toward us, I did as Freya instructed.

I was free of the hammock-man, but I didn't want to go home. I didn't want to be alone with my mind full of these new troubling thoughts. I found myself walking to the edge of the park, with a sliver-moon above. Soon I was staring into the wall of gray human homes, with their amber-colored windows and black human silhouettes. I wondered if they knew all this—that they were on an island, far away from everything else. I assumed they did. They had chosen this place. Why?

I ran to the ocean and looked out at the waves coming and coming at me. The froth rushed to me on its billion tiny white legs and then crumbled to nothing. I looked into the slate-blue night and felt a simmering rage within me. The Bison knew all

about this but hadn't told me. They knew that not only were they penned inside a park in a city, but that this city was only one of a billion cities, this one far from anything—some tiny insignificant island far from anything that mattered.

TWENTY-FIVE

In the morning, amid the catapulting confusion of my mind, I had no choice but to do my rounds. I was still the Eyes.

It seemed to be a quiet day in the park, with very few people out and about. This was a workday for the humans, so most were in their boxes sitting still, looking into blue lights, not walking and riding and dancing in the park. It was cold and windy outside, too, a state of affairs that happens often here, given the park's proximity to the sea.

So on this windy and cloudy day I raced through the park, past the peanut-pond and through the eucalyptus forest and past the lime-green waterfall and I saw nothing unusual, nothing to upset the Equilibrium.

I was running close to the speed of light, passing by the plaza, when something caught my eye. It was a rectangle on a stick

stuck into the grass, and in the rectangle was a dog. A picture of a dog. A dog that looked like me.

My friends had told me about these pictures but until now, I had not wholly appreciated the strangeness of seeing one myself. There were words around the picture, and though I cannot read, the meaning seemed clear. The sign was telling people to look out for this dog. This dog that I deduced was me. Startled and unnerved, I ran quickly away from the sign, only to encounter another one just up the way from the first one.

It was the same sign. Same words, same dog. I ran again, this time cutting through the forest near the plaza so I could get to the other side. I suppose there was part of me that hoped the signs were only in the plaza—only pertaining to that one side of one part of the park.

But when I broke through the forest and into the clearing on the other side of the plaza, I saw another sign. Another me in the rectangle. And now I added the clues up and the truth seemed undeniable. These signs were warning people about me. They were telling people I was dangerous, or a fugitive of some kind, or worse. Could these signs be telling people to catch me, to kill me?

"There you are!"

It was a voice above me, and sounded like Yolanda. I looked up to see that it was, indeed, Yolanda. She was floating near me,

as if she might land on top of me. I am always a bit concerned that because Yolanda's landings are so chaotic—so much wing and beak and bone—that she will land on top of me. She has never done this, I should note. And this time was like all the others: she landed and gave me nothing more than the gentle breath of her folding wings.

"Did you see the signs?" she asked.

I told her I did, and before I could express my bewilderment at being represented all over these signs, all over the park, she said something strange.

"No, no," she said. "These are new. These are different. These say that there's a *coyote* in the park."

"Is that really what the signs say?" I asked.

"Yup, look," she said, and swept her gray wing under a series of symbols—apparently those that meant *coyote*. Yolanda knew I could not read, knew that only *she* could read, and yet she seemed to hold out hope, eternal hope, that by occasionally pointing to some collection of symbols we'd suddenly learn to read as she could. It was a little bit irritating, to be honest.

"Ah," I said, and nodded. She smiled.

I was very intrigued by this new development—the possible existence of one or more coyotes in the park. I had heard of coyotes, but only as a long-ago species. Coyotes were known as a mangy and troublesome and even dangerous kind, and as far as I'd known, they had been driven out by the humans thousands of years ago.

"So you haven't seen one?" Yolanda asked. It took me a moment to realize that this put in question my competence as the Eyes. If the humans, being so clumsy and oblivious, had seen coyotes before I had, what credibility could I claim?

"I haven't," I said. I could not lie. I will not lie.

"Well, I guess we have to be on the lookout," she said, and then, with a few flaps of her heavy wings, she drifted off.

I was left a bit stunned, thinking that an entirely new—or old!—kind of animal was among us. A dangerous and troublesome sort of animal that looked, from a distance, a bit like myself. It was all very confusing.

"There he is!" said a voice.

It was a Parks Person on a bicycle. She was riding toward me, with a second Parks Person riding a bit behind her. The first one pedaled toward me, and I had to chuckle briefly to myself, because they seemed to think they would catch me by simply riding toward me. These people!

Ha ha hoooooo!

They do make me laugh. Bicycles are funny jokes to me. They give me laughs and chuckles and sometimes even giggles. Bicycles are as statues are to rockets, with me being the rocket.

Now the two bicycle-people were getting off their machines. They believed they had caught up to me due to their great speed.

Oh! Oh the hilarity. Ha ha hoooooo!

Now they were coming at me from either side, slowly, with their arms out like those of crabs. It really was sad, how much they really believed they could capture me this way, two people with their slow legs and little hands and their shiny mushroom-hats on their heads.

I waited. Because I am mischievous with creatures who think they are fast, sometimes I wait until they are close to me. To tease them. To make them feel they have a chance. In this case I waited until I could feel the heat from their little hands and could see their wide-open eyes. They were so excited!

Then I bolted. They blinked and I was a hundred feet away, laughing to myself, shaking my head.

"Where is he?" the one asked.

"Over there," the other said.

"How'd he get over there? He was just here!"

These people. These people! They blinked again and I was away again, double the distance.

Oh I have fun. I have fun with people like this.

And then the first one spoke into a black device for a time, and then the two of them got back on their bicycles and headed toward me again. It was funny! It really was.

But one can only play with such people for so long. And there is always the outside possibility that such play would bring about more Control-the-Animals people, and possibly unusual

or new weapons, and anyway, I had things to do. I owed the Bison an update soon, and I had yet to see what was happening with the goats—a topic about which they would want updated information.

When I got near the windmill, as I was slowing from light speed to mortal speed, I could see the vast mass of hair that was the goat army. They were eating just as they were eating the day before, all of their heads down and their jaws pumping and their eyes dead to all other stimuli. The day was overcast and windy, but there was one shaft of light just then as I approached, and this one shaft of light ended on the silvery-gray back of a certain goat, who was away from the rest, and who was looking exactly at me.

"Hello," she said.

I could not believe she could see me. I was a hundred miles away or so, and I was hidden amid a blackberry thicket and beyond a forest of redwoods.

"I see you," she said.

I decided to emerge.

"You weren't very well hidden," she said, which normally would have stung—would have pierced my heart—but there was such good cheer in her voice, such gentleness and humor, that I found myself smiling. She was so immediately appealing that I couldn't help asking her why she was so far from the rest of her group, eating all alone. She said her name was Helene. I had never heard this

name before, but it sounded both regal and smooth like a trickle of warm water, and thus far she herself seemed both regal and smooth like warm water. So why was she so apart and so alone?

"Oh gosh," she said, "they wouldn't want to talk to *me*! I don't blame them. Look at me. I'm a freak!"

I looked at her carefully. To me she looked like all the other goats, and I told her so.

"You don't have to be polite," she said. "I'm used to scaring everyone around me. I'm horrible. A monster. A blight."

Again I told her I couldn't figure out what it was that she thought so unusual or frightening in her appearance.

"Um," she said, "for starters, my horns?" She tilted her head to me to afford me a better look.

I examined them closely and still saw nothing out of the ordinary.

"Oh!" she said, laughing. "I forgot you don't have goats here. And maybe you're not so good at observation?"

Now it was me who had to laugh. She didn't know I was the Eyes! This was very funny to me so I allowed myself a good long chuckle while shaking my head.

Ha ha hoooooo!

"What's funny?" she asked. Before I answered, I had to do one last ha ha hoooooo! just to demonstrate the ridiculousness of her suggesting I was not so good at observation, which was evidence that *she* was not so good at observation!

I had to tell her, as humbly as I could, that I was not only good at observation, but that I was so good that I was basically in charge of all seeing in the park.

"Well congratulations," she said, and seemed very sincere in saying it. "That sounds like a lot of responsibility."

I nodded, grateful she recognized this.

"But your powers of observation," she said, "make it all the more puzzling that you can't see my glaring defects."

"I have to say," I said, "there is nothing much different about your horns. Every other goat I've seen has two, and they're all basically the same color, and they curl away from your heads the same way, and they get pointy at the ends. I've observed this about all of your horns, I've compared and contrasted, and they're all basically the same."

She scoffed. She really did. I was beginning to like her, then she scoffed. Scoffing is not the sound a friend makes.

"But you left out the most important part," she said, smiling in a way that made me feel a little silly. "It's not the length, or the curvature, or the color that matters," she said. "It's the forma-tion of the *cross-lines*."

It took her some time to explain this in a way that allows me to explain it to you. Apparently, in the world of goats, there are lines that go horizontally across each horn, and to goats, the pattern of these lines is of great importance. The best kinds of lines, Helene

told me, are both wavy and parallel. The next-best kinds are straight and parallel. "Parallel is just the baseline for normalcy," she said.

Now I looked closely at Helene's horns. The lines on hers were not parallel. Some were wavy, and some straight, and some loopy, and some were even crisscrossed. But even after I noticed these differences, I backed up for a second and could barely see any lines at all.

"Now you can imagine the horror I inflict on others when they see me," Helene said. "They tell me about this horror, all the time. So I try to stay out of the way, so as to cause as little suffering as possible."

I thought about this as I headed home. I had never known anyone who had these sorts of thoughts about themselves, these low opinions about some aspect of their physical form, these odd ideas about the right kinds of stripes on one's horns. I thought about how I might convince Helene that she looked fine, that she looked like every other goat. Or rather, she seemed to me to be just the right amount of different from every other goat.

I made my way through the park, avoiding the roads, avoiding the well-trod paths and absolutely avoiding the plaza, until I finally arrived home, only to find my home had become a wall.

It was a wall!

A human had done this. That much I knew. The hole in the tree where I entered my home was now a wall of gray cement. I had seen this before. Many years ago. When the Control-the-Animals people or the Parks People wanted to close off a hollow, they did this. I remembered there was a small, very small, hollow of a tree where humans would put garbage, and eventually that hollow was made into a cement wall.

But that had been so long ago.

And no humans knew of my hollow.

Except apparently they did.

I sat and looked at this wall for some time, knowing that it was impenetrable but also not believing that my home was no longer available to me. That it had ended. That my hollow was now a wall.

Only occasionally have I felt real anger toward humans. I felt it toward Twisty, my captor, and once or twice I have felt it toward the drivers of vehicles who drive recklessly, who endanger us animals and also their fellow humans.

But I have never felt real anger toward the humans who work in this park. They seem to love the park like we love the park. But this was cruel. It was intentional. They knew an animal lived in this hollow. They must know that animals live in hollows! And still they made my home into a wall.

Why?

TWENTY-SIX

I thought about who lived closest. It was Sonja, who lived just down the hill. I went to her and even before I announced myself she had clambered out of her burrow and had come to me, rubbing sleep from her eye.

"I smelled you and heard you," she said groggily, "and I saw what they did. I'm so sorry. It must have been today."

Until that moment it hadn't occurred to me that they had done this in the last few hours. It had to be. How had they known I would be gone?

"It's a nasty thing," she said. "Nasty and brutish."

I had never heard her so passionate. Her anger made me feel good. I can't explain it. It's like she took the fire inside me, put it in a torch, and then set it between us. It was no longer just mine.

"Tonight sleep here," she said. "There's plenty of room."

When I looked doubtful, she pushed some eucalyptus leaves out of the way to reveal that her dugout was vast—interrupted only by sticks and logs that we shoved away to make room.

That night I slept fitfully. I was used to the smell of my own home, my own things, and Sonja's dwelling was cleaner than mine, and smelled only of dirt and Sonja herself. While my nose tried to get used to this clean-Sonja smell, my mind was darting around, thinking of the terrible thing the humans had done to my home, and about the coyote or coyotes who might be roaming our park. In all my millions of days, so much had never happened in so short a span. I was dizzy and dazed and did not find rest till the night's smallest hours.

At first light I snuck out, careful not to wake Sonja, and I ran to the ocean, wanting space, wanting light and air. I sprinted on the beach, helping the world turn, and when I was tired I jogged across the road to the windmill, looking for the goats and specifically for Helene.

I found her, as I had before, alone.

"Oh hi!" she said when she saw me. She had a beautiful voice, musical like birdsong, crisp like fresh rain.

I looked around and noticed that the endless expanse of weeds was just about gone. "Did you goats eat all of this?" I asked.

"Oh sure," she said. "And we've actually been going sort of slow compared to usual. The prickly weeds take a bit longer than the non-prickly weeds. You should see us go at those! You're up early. Any special reason?"

There was something so open about her, her eyes so warm and her voice so clear, that I told her about my hollow becoming a wall, and by the end my voice was breaking and my throat was closing and my eyes were wet and I was angry at myself for letting all of these things happen. But she looked at me with great kindness and just the right amount of annoyance.

"That is just awful," she said. "Who would do such a thing?"

"Some humans, I assume," I said.

"Well, that is unacceptable," she said. "Just unacceptable. Though I suppose I don't have a home, either."

She told me that she and her fellow goats were shuttled from place to place, and usually slept in the open air, and that as far as she could remember, she'd rarely, if ever, slept in the same place twice.

Now it was my turn to think something was unacceptable.

"But it's what I'm used to," she said. "The adventure of new places, new sights, makes it worthwhile."

The thought of new places got me thinking about the Bison, and I told Helene about my plan to free them.

"Bison, eh?" she said. "I've seen Bison. I remember one time traveling on a train for many days, and when we stopped, we were

in a vast plain ringed by snowy mountains. And all around us were Bison. They are picky eaters."

There was so much in what she said, so many revelations and mysteries, that I paused for a moment to take them in. First, she said she had seen Bison, many Bison, somewhere other than here, and that took my breath away. I had only known the three Bison here, so had never considered the possibility that there could be more, many more, somewhere across the sea. And they lived where? In a *vast plain ringed by snowy mountains?*

I did not know this word, *snowy*, and asked her about it. She explained snow—not that it made any sense, really; it seemed so silly and unnecessary and weird—and then, once she was done, I realized I didn't know what the word *mountain* meant, either.

"A mountain is like a rock, but a hundred thousand times bigger," she said, and this made little sense to me, either. She seemed to know I was confused.

"You see that boulder over there?" she asked, and nodded to the great boulder on the beach, which served as the end point of the sand as we knew it. I'd never been beyond this boulder, actually. It was jagged and steep and there seemed to be no point in climbing it—especially given it was covered in bird feces.

"Well," Helene said, "a mountain is like that boulder, but so much huger. If it took you ten seconds to climb that boulder, it would take you ten days to climb a mountain."

This to me made sense. Much of what Helene said made sense, and opened my eyes—so much so that I spent every day with her for some time, listening and asking questions and hearing her talk about things like deserts and lakes and creatures I'd never heard of and scarcely believed. She described animals with impossible combinations of fur and hooves and horns, and in numbers that overwhelmed my mind. Everything she said about the main-land made it seem that not only were we on an island, but we were on a very *small* island, which contained only a fraction of things that existed in the world.

Helene described these things casually, never allowing me to feel ignorant, and when I told her stories of the park, she listened closely and asked very good questions, laughing and oohing at all the right times. She was a very good talker and a very good listener, and I have to admit I drank from her mind as I would a perfect spring after a long hot day.

For the next dozen days, I was still doing my rounds, and still reported to the Bison each day, but afterward I would return to Helene to hear more about all I did not know. And because I no longer had a home, these nights I slept near Helene. She had a knack for choosing spots under the brambly trees that kept us warm from the ocean breeze, and we talked until we fell asleep. Then, almost immediately I would go on dreaming of all she'd said.

The next day, we'd begin again. Usually, at some point while we talked, I would catch a familiar shadow crossing over us, and I knew it was Bertrand. He would fly over us, high above, and I knew he saw us. Each time I would look up to him, and tell him to come say hello, to chat with me and Helene—for I wanted very much for him to hear all I was hearing, to share his own stories with her—but each time, the moment I invited him to join us, he would glide away like he hadn't heard me. It was very unusual behavior for Bertrand, and I planned to ask him about it someday.

On one of these occasions, when I was looking up at Bertrand's retreating silhouette, Helene saw my eyes to the sky and she smiled. "You like the Sun?" she asked.

I found this to be a very strange question, one I had never heard. The Sun was the beginning of everything in the world, and gave me life and gave life to all I knew, so yes, I thought, I like the Sun. What's not to like?

"Of course I like the Sun," I said. "Actually I love the Sun. The Sun is God."

She laughed.

I mentioned that Helene scoffed once before, and scoffing is not the sound a friend makes. But this, this laugh, was worse. By this time I liked Helene a great deal, and found her to be a fount of knowledge and spectacular stories, but her ability to make these mean sounds was a distinct problem.

"I'm sorry," she said. "Did you say that the Sun was God?"

"Well, yes," I said. "And clouds are her messengers."

"You don't say!" she said. "And what about rain?"

"Rain is only rain," I said. All this was so elementary to me that I felt, for a moment, that Helene was joking with me. How could she not know these things? Island or main-land, these facts were foundational.

Helene looked up at the Sun, wearing an enigmatic smile.

"If you say so," she said, and went back to eating. I watched her chew for ten or so heartbeats, and then had to press her.

"You don't think the Sun is God?" I asked.

"Well, this is the first I've heard that," she said, which seemed to me an impossibility. "But you could be right! Maybe it *is* God. Either way seems good."

I didn't know where to start. Helene was referring to the Sun as *it* instead of *she*, which was very bothersome to me. But more annoying than that was this bizarre idea, expressed so blithely, that the Sun was not God. Or that such an undebatable fact of existence was a maybe-yes, maybe-no question, like whether or not ducks were reliable or pupusas were delicious.

"Are you saying," I said, "that there's a fiery orb in the sky that gives us all life, but that she isn't God? That she's just some random ball of fire?"

Now Helene stopped eating and looked warmly up at me. "You're probably right," she said. "It's just not a topic I've thought that much about. It could be that the sun is God and makes everything nice and good. Or it could be that the sun is just like me or you or that boulder with the bird feces on it."

"Just another thing?" I asked. I was so baffled and offended I could barely form words.

"Right," she said, oblivious to my baffled state. "Not that it's not important. It is! But the rest of all we know and see is important, too. The ocean. The air. The land. The trees and sand and stones. Even the worms! All things equal and equally important." And again, as if she'd been talking about food or fungus, she went back to eating. Then another voice was heard.

"Who are you talking to, Strange-Stripes?" This was the voice of another goat, who seemed to be on the other side of a thick bush. His tone was mocking.

"A friend," Helene said to the voice on the other side of the bush. Then she turned to me and whispered, "Is it okay that I called you a friend?"

And even though she had just said a bunch of things that rattled my mind and caused me some confusion and even hurt feelings, I very much liked Helene and yes, considered her a friend. A new friend, which is a very exciting kind of friend. So

in answer to her question, I wanted to say *Of course!* And *Yes!* And *Your voice fills me with happiness!* And *You fill me with images of freedom and adventure!*

But I only said, "Yeah, sure."

Now a second voice came from the bush.

"Strange-Stripes has a friend? This I have to see." This second voice seemed very unpleasant—more unpleasant than the first. And even more unpleasant was realizing that the other goats called my friend Helene by this ugly name, Strange-Stripes.

Now there was a rustling in the bush, which I took to mean that these two unpleasant goats were actually coming around to get a look at me, this new friend of Helene's. I was ready to stand my ground when they saw me, but I was also a bit afraid they would say mean things to me, too. When they came around the bush, though, they immediately lowered their eyes and knelt like I was a king.

"Sir!" one goat said. I was almost sure he was talking to me.

"So sorry, sir!" the other said. I was almost sure this second one was talking to me, too. They were very deferential. It felt so odd, but also sort of good, having these recently cruel goats suddenly so worshipful and meek. I looked over to Helene, whose mouth had formed itself into the slightest smirk.

"We didn't realize who we were talking to," the first goat said.

"The shrubbery was in our way," the second said. "We really meant no offense, sir. Your Sirness. Your Powerfulness. Sorry."

"We really meant no disrespect," the first added. "It was a very thick sort of shrubbery."

I will explain.

These goats, and most goats, are herd animals. They clump together and move as a group. And they usually have a different creature that moves them around, guides them and shoos them and basically tells them where to go. And these moving-around creatures are of two types: humans and dogs.

I am a dog. You know this. So when these two goats saw me, they snapped in line. They bowed down. They were ready to obey. Which meant that the rest of the goats would do the same. I didn't need them to snap in line or bow down or anything like that, but to have them treat Helene with dignity? I had that power.

There are times in this life when I have been surprised by the words I say. The words that I should be wholly aware of and in control of. But sometimes they seem to be channeled from some other place—from the sky, from the past, from a nobler version of myself. And such a group of words came from my mouth at that moment.

I said, "You disappoint me."

I said this to the cruel goats who were sneering and snickering at my friend Helene. And then I stared at them for a very long

time. Oh the looks in their eyes! It was something like terror, something like apology, something like shame.

"We are so sorry," one of them said.

"We are embarrassed," the other said.

Out of the corner of my eye I could see Helene. Her eyes were a thousand times bigger than before—she couldn't believe what she was seeing and hearing.

"I think you can do better," I said to the goats, and immediately they nodded so vigorously I feared their heads would fall from their necks.

"Thank you, sir," one said. "For taking the time to educate us."

"And for your faith in us," said another.

And then I went further, and even while saying these next words, I worried I was going far too far.

"Henceforth, among your kind, there will be no differentiation based on tiny deviations of physical form. There will be no snickering based on things like the sort of cross-stripes one of you has or doesn't have, or the direction one's fur goes, or the color of your eyes or hooves. Such behavior is an affront to the dignity of your species. Is that understood?"

The two goats before me nodded gravely, and I looked beyond them to see that a crowd of other goats had heard, too, and were fixed in place, grave agreement in their eyes.

I couldn't think of anything else to say, so I said, "Now go forth and eat some weeds."

TWENTY-SEVEN

The next day, after we woke up and after Helene had spent a hundred or so hours eating, her eyes brightened.

"I almost forgot to tell you!" she said. "In the middle of the night, I had an idea for you."

The Sun had recently risen with her billion golden arms, and I will admit that I worried Helene would tell me unsettling ideas about the Sun not being God. I worried Helene would tell me that ants were God, or mushrooms, or some other upside-down notion. But instead, she had a question that was very good, and an idea that was even better.

"You were saying yesterday that you were planning to free the Bison," she said. "But where will you bring them once they're free of their fencing?"

This I didn't know. It was one of the things I hadn't worked out. The farthest I'd taken the plan was to the sea. I kept picturing

them on the sand, running free, but that's where the dream ended, and I told her so.

"Hm," she said, and looked out to the roiling ocean. "Well, I'm so grateful to you for sticking up for me with the other goats—I can't tell you how grateful—so I was up half the night thinking of how to repay you."

I told her it was wholly unnecessary that she repay me. She grinned.

"I knew you would say that," she said, "but anyway. In the middle of the night I had a thought! Why not bring the Bison on the ship? Back to the main-land! Where we'll go, there's more than enough room for all the Bison in the world. There's a billion miles where they can run and graze and sleep—and even hide, if they need to. The land never ends. I've lived there all my life and haven't seen even a tiny part of it."

Immediately this idea seemed a perfect one to me. An idea so flawless and inevitable I knew we had to make it real. But would the ship really be big enough? How would the Bison not be seen and expelled?

"Good questions," she said. "It'll be tricky, because they're so large. I assume your Bison pals are large?"

I confirmed to Helene that they were very large.

"Well," she said, "the thought I had was that maybe they could mix in with all of us, especially if we were jumping around

and on each other's backs, which we do sometimes. And when we all tramp up the gangway onto the ship, your Bison friends could sneak in there among us and maybe they wouldn't get noticed." Helene closed her eyes, as if picturing it. She nodded at the sight in her mind. "It's an idea, anyway."

Now she looked out at the innumerable goats, of all colors, and I did, too. I wondered if the Bison could possibly blend in among them. There were some larger goats, but even the largest among them was less than half the size of Meredith, the smallest of the Bison. But we could work on it, I thought.

"Well, it'll take a lot of planning—a hundred years of planning—but I know it will work." I told her she was quite brilliant, and told her I was very grateful, and told her that tomorrow I would tell the Assistant Eyes about the plan, and if they liked it, a few days later I would tell the Bison, and then we would begin drawing up schemes. I was going on and on and that's when Helene stopped me.

"We don't have a hundred years to plan this," she said. "We don't even have a hundred days or a hundred hours. The boat leaves tomorrow morning. At seven-oh-eight."

TWENTY-EIGHT

And then I was running. I was running because there was little time to plan all of this, make all of this happen, and I was running because at that moment I couldn't look at Helene. She was my new and very good friend, a friend who opened my mind and filled it with new treasures, and now she was leaving. The thought hit me like a thousand-foot-tall wave with all its chaos and cruelty.

But more important than my sadness about losing this friend was the possibility—the inevitability!—of freeing the Bison. Helene's plan was the most sparkling and logical and inspiring plan we could ever conjure. And so I ran to spread the word. In my history of running fast, this was far and away the fastest I have been. I pierced the air like a knife thrown, I bent the trees, I created a vacuum that threatened to suck the clouds from the sky.

I ran to gather the Assistants for an emergency meeting and succeeded in seconds. I told everyone to meet me at the top of the rock and they hustled to do just this, everyone but Bertrand. I could not find Bertrand. But we could not wait. I assumed he would hear or would fly over and find us soon enough. In the meantime we needed to move ahead.

"Seven-oh-eight," I said to Angus. "Is this something related to time? Helene said that's when the ship leaves."

"Yes," Angus said with great seriousness and pride in his time-telling. "That means the morning. Not long from now."

I told the Assistant Eyes that all the vague plans we'd made to free the Bison would have to move up, would have to come into sharp focus immediately. We'd have to plan and practice all day and night, and be ready to free them at dawn, to get them on the boat well before this seven-oh-eight. It was the only way. This was our first and last chance to set them free—not just free to run on the beach for a moment, but free forever.

"That is a lot to take in," Angus said.

"My brain is vibrating," Yolanda said.

"I like it," Sonja said. "I think it can work."

I was surprised by Sonja's confident tone, and everyone else was, too. I don't think anyone was doubting that we should free them, or that this was a good opportunity to do that,

but Sonja was the first to give this new and precious chance momentum.

"We need to start now," she said. I loved her for that. Sometimes in this life so much depends on one friend simply saying, *Yes, we must do this.*

Or *Yes, I see it that way, too.*

Or *It is high time we do something great and grand.*

Now, with that simple statement, the fact of us doing this, of freeing the Bison the next morning, became real. Now it was just a matter of directing every fiber of our being and every moment from now till then to the task.

So it was easy!

But also not so easy.

It was one of those instances where it's so complicated that it's simple, because we knew how complicated it would be, and that idea was simple enough.

I said all this to the Assistants, and they looked at me with blank stares. I realized that when I'd shared this notion with Bertrand, it had made perfect sense.

"Anyway," Angus said. "We have less than twenty-four hours." Everyone's stares were still blank, but this blankness was now directed at Angus, not me, for which I was grateful. "Less than a day," he clarified, and we went to work.

I had wanted to make sure the Assistants agreed with the plan before I brought it to the Bison, and now I felt ready. I came to their enclosure and found them surrounded by humans. More than I had ever seen in their midst before. Some I recognized, some I didn't. There were ten or more. They had equipment. Tools. Poles, ropes, little silver discs and little black boxes. What were they doing?

I couldn't get close.

Something about the Bison being surrounded by humans with their tools made me all the more determined to set them loose. And so the rest of the daylight hours were busy with the Assistants and me meeting and planning and convincing.

With Angus, we convinced the raccoons to help, which wasn't very difficult, for they liked nothing better than mischief at the expense of humans. And honestly, I think they were happy to shift the focus from the museum break-in plan, which they never loved.

With Yolanda's help we met with the pelicans, twenty or more of them, to work out their role—mostly one of observation and possible misdirection. She also gathered the gulls, who were skeptical about the feasibility of the plan, but who agreed to go along. There is something about an urgent task that unites and inspires. No one said no to us, except of course the ducks.

It was Sonja's idea to ask the ducks. I had insisted there was no point, and Angus and Yolanda agreed. There was nothing ducks could do that gulls could not do, so why ask the ducks in the first place? Why risk them mucking up the plan as only ducks can do? Yolanda and Angus would not take part in the asking of the ducks; exasperated, they went off to clear their heads.

And there we were, Sonja and me with the ducks, standing on the edge of their smelly pond as they swam about, barely paying attention to us. When finally they noticed us standing at the water's edge, waiting to be noticed, one of them swam over.

"What's all this about?" said this one, their leader. His name was Jerome.

I told him that we planned to free the Bison.

"Who are the Bison?" said another duck. This one's name was Jerry. All the ducks' names start with J. It's one of the many, many upsetting things about the ducks. Not that there is anything wrong with this J-sound—it is a fine sound!—but all animals of a species should not have to adhere to one starting letter. It is bad form, against all the laws of nature and good taste.

Anyway, we explained who the Bison were. I don't know how the ducks did not know who the Bison were, but nothing about the ducks surprised me.

"So what did you say you're doing with them?" Jerome asked.

"We're freeing them," I said.

"From what? They're not free?" Jerome said.

"They're stuck inside a fence," we told him.

Jerome's head was suddenly underwater, so I didn't know if he heard me or not. He popped up again, but then Jerry's head went under.

"Tell me again, when is this happening?" Jerome asked.

"Early tomorrow morning," I said.

"Oh, the morning is a busy time for us," he said, and ducked his head underwater again. Jerry reappeared.

"Very busy," he said. "We have to swim in the morning, and periodically put our heads underwater. This is key." And *he* popped *his* head underwater. But Jerome was back.

"Such a busy time," Jerome said.

Another duck's head popped out of the smelly green water.

"What are we talking about?" she asked. This one's name was Jackie.

"These guys want to free the squirrels," Jerome told her.

"Not the squirrels," I said. "The Bison."

"Why would they want to free the squirrels?" Jackie asked. "The squirrels seem pretty free to me."

"Bison," I said. "We're trying to free the *Bison*."

"Bison!" Jerome said. "Are those the big guys inside the fence? Who says they want to be free?"

"We did. And they did," I said. I tried to explain that their wanting to be free was not part of the debate, that we were actually hoping to get the ducks' *help* in freeing them, but they continued to jabber among themselves.

"Why wouldn't they just fly over the fence?" Jackie asked.

"I don't think they can fly," Jerome said.

"Sure they can!" Jackie insisted. "I see them flying all the time! They are white and fluffy and fly sort of slowly."

"Oh, right!" Jerome said.

"I think you're talking about clouds," Jerry said.

"No, we were talking about squirrels," Jackie said.

"Bison," Jerome corrected.

"What are we talking about again?" said a fourth duck, this one named Jeremiah. "My beak is itchy."

And at that, we felt it was time to leave. We turned away, and I heard one of the ducks say, "Who was that?"

The answer was "No idea."

When we were out of earshot, I told Sonja we should not have asked the ducks. No serious plan ever involves ducks. Finally she agreed, though she seemed bewildered and disappointed that the ducks could not be inspired.

But we did need the rats, the crows, and the horses. So we made arrangements with all of them, and to the last creature they were excited about the plan, and about freeing the Bison, and were quite happy to do it as soon as possible.

After all our gatherings and plannings, I was so tired I needed some time at the top of the rock, for air and contemplation.

"Don't worry," Sonja said. She had come up next to me. This time she'd approached with confidence, with directness, without any of the shyness I'd known her for. I have to say the transformation was remarkable and I was very proud of her. Even her busted eye looked better; it seemed to have turned itself into a handsome scar, a dignified thing.

"We're making good progress," she said. "I even think the ducks will surprise you in the end. I think everyone has a role to play."

I sighed the loudest sigh of my life. Again with the ducks.

"And also," she said, "you know there's been talk about who will oversee things in the park when the Bison are gone."

I hadn't had time to think about this. Yes, when the Bison were gone, they would leave a void—a rather large one. Some group or some *one* would have to step in and become the leader, the overseer, the Keeper of the Equilibrium.

"It could be you," Sonja said. "Think of it. You're already the closest to the Bison. You know all that they know. In fact, you've delivered all the information they have. So it just seems natural that you'd take over when they're gone."

This I hadn't thought of.

In fact, never in ten thousand years would I have thought of such a thing. Me as the Keeper of the Equilibrium?

Sonja must have seen the astonishment on my face.

"But who else could it be?" she asked.

And though I was flattered to be thought of this way, and could see the logic, given my proximity to the Bison, all I could think of was Bertrand. He was the one I went to for wisdom. Could I be the Keeper of the Equilibrium when I looked to someone else for guidance?

I thought about this as we crisscrossed the park, making our final arrangements for the Bison's escape. There were routes to clear. There were animals to warn. There were humans to count. There were distractions to design. And there were goats to engage.

TWENTY-NINE

I had made a plan with Helene to talk to the goats once their day was done. It was just before sunset when I went to the windmill and found them all still eating, their heads down and jaws churning. Helene led me to a hill overlooking the field of flowers and weeds, though the weeds were nearly gone. Not one of the goats looked up.

"Just bark," Helene said.

"Bark?" I asked.

"Do you know how to bark?" she asked. "Usually the dogs will bark."

I had only barked a few times in my life. Being the Eyes required speed and stealth, and barking eliminated both, really. Barking brought attention to oneself, and slowed one down considerably. You can't run so fast while barking. Not everyone knows that.

But I understood her meaning. I needed to make some sound so the goats would take notice. And only a few of them had seen me, ever, so I figured a very loud first impression might be in order.

"Yip," I said.

Or I thought I said "Yip," but even Helene, who was standing next to me, didn't seem to hear it. The wind from the ocean was strong, so I thought my "Yip" had gotten lost in the offshore breeze. I tried another yip, this one louder. This time, Helene took notice, but also smiled a pained sort of smile, as if to tell me my yip was more like a ^{yip}. I had to do much, much better. I decided to just go big and bark.

So I sucked the wind from the ocean.

And I ate the clouds from the sky.

And I looked to the Sun and gathered from her all the strength she had to give.

And I roared a kind of bark that was also a howl and also a bellow and even a bit of a squall. I had my eyes closed as I unleashed it, and when it ended I opened my eyes to find a thousand goat heads and two thousand goat eyes looking up at me, terrified. I had no idea what to say to them.

But Helene did. "In the morning..." she whispered to me.

"In the morning!" I roared.

"We will engage in a heroic act..." Helene whispered.

"We will engage in a heroic act!" I roared.

Already I saw that these were the right words. The goats, who I took to be only interested in eating prickly leaves, seemed very interested in the words *heroic act*.

"We will cloak and free three animal captives..." Helene whispered.

"We will cloak and free three animal captives!" I roared.

I repeated her words for a bit, and soon enough I had gained confidence and momentum enough to lay out the plan. The work of the goats was not so complicated, I should say. They merely had to surround the Bison, leaping and baying and generally making chaos all around, so the humans minding them would have trouble seeing the Bison in their midst.

By the end of our gathering, I was convinced that the goats would perform their duties with passion and determination. The rest would be up to the gulls, the pelicans, the rats and raccoons, the squirrels and the horses—with absolutely nothing being done, please and thank you, by the ducks.

The only problem with any of this was that we had not yet found an opening to tell the Bison about the soon-ness of their escape. All day, the Bison had been surrounded by those new humans in official-seeming clothes with all their new tools. Every so often Yolanda would fly overhead to see if anything had changed, if the

humans had left, and it wasn't until deep in the evening that she reported that the Bison were again alone.

"We heard," Freya said to me when I finally snuck into the enclosure. All three Bison were in the corner farthest from the human-made parts of their world. "And we are ready."

"We are so ready," Meredith added.

The humans had spent the day measuring and weighing and poking the Bison.

"It was humiliating," Samuel said.

"Degrading," Meredith said.

"These were new people, from a university of some kind," Freya said. I did not know what a university was, so I said nothing. But I saw that Freya was both depleted and very angry. I had never seen her so angry.

"The usual Parks People treat us kindly," she said. "We have known them for many years. In most cases, we have been here far longer than them, so there is a respect there. A respect for one's elders. But these new people—to them we were just things. Rocks to turn over and inspect."

"Things to poke and prod," Samuel said.

"So we are ready to go," Freya said again.

I was thrilled to hear this, so we went over the plan, which both Freya and Meredith found reasonable and plausible. Samuel was not optimistic about its likelihood of success, but I had anticipated his

dour outlook. As long as Freya and Meredith were for it, though, it would happen, and Samuel would go along. Freya had told me many times that Samuel would do anything to avoid being alone.

"Now Johannes," Freya said, her eyes suddenly intense and upon me. "When we're gone, I would like you to take over. I would like you to be the Keeper of the Equilibrium. Would you do that?"

I could not respond. There had been no buildup, no preamble. But Sonja had been right.

"I know it's quite a bit of responsibility," she said. "But you are the clear choice. You have been essential to our work, and you've been privy to our deliberations and judgments. You are younger than we are, of course, but we have every faith in you."

"We really do," Meredith added. She smiled at me through watery eyes. "You'll do well."

Samuel said nothing, and finally Meredith turned to him, annoyed. "Now would be the appropriate time for you to offer some encouragement."

"Well," he muttered, "there really wasn't anyone else."

I accepted.

I would be the Keeper.

"But when can we talk about all I need to know?" I asked.

There were so many thousands of things to ask, and there was nowhere near enough time.

"My son," Freya said. "You have been the Eyes for a long, long time. There is nothing left for you to know."

And though I did not believe this, I accepted her verdict. I had no choice.

Samuel gave her an imploring look, and Freya looked down, then at me. "There is one more thing," she said.

"Yes?" I said.

"You're half-coyote," she said.

"Okay, sounds good," I said, because I had not heard her correctly.

"No," she said, her voice firm. "Listen to me carefully. Your father was a coyote."

I laughed. I laughed because it was such a stupid thing for them to say—to say such a terrible thing at a time like this, when we had so much planning to do.

"I'm sorry, son," Freya said. "Maybe we should have told you sooner."

"I told you we should have told him sooner," Samuel said.

I couldn't speak. What Freya had said didn't make sense.

"Think about it," she said. "Why do you think you're so fast? Why do you think the other dogs look at you like you're different, like you're similar but radically apart?"

My throat dried. My eyes swam.

"Why do you suppose you make the unusual sounds you do? Do you know any other dogs who say ha ha hooooo?"

As you know, I had always thought all these things were due to me being a free dog. A fast dog. An extraordinary dog.

"This is what a coyote says," she said. "This is the sound your father made. We loved that sound." She looked to Samuel and Meredith, who both smiled. I could tell their minds had journeyed far into the past.

"Your father was the last coyote on this island," Samuel finally said. "When he died, all that was left of his kind was you."

Oh how my mind spun! For a moment I believed them, then I did not believe them, no. They were old and their minds were not sharp. This could be some sort of dream-thought of theirs, some strange error of fading minds.

"He was quite majestic," Meredith said.

"I had no plans to ever tell you," Freya said, "because it would not help you to know. It would only endanger you, really. It was better for you to think you were all-dog. But now that the humans are looking for a coyote, you should know."

"They're looking for *you*," Samuel said.

THIRTY

I ran. By now the sky was black and the Sun's million siblings were out and shimmering, and I ran from the Bison and to Bertrand. I had to see him, to tell him this news, to see if he thought it could be true. If he *knew* it to be true. Oh, I thought, I don't know if I could bear it if he knew, too!

I ran in the silver light, so angry, but then I remembered I had happy news, too. I would be Keeper of the Equilibrium! I was furious that I had never known about my blood, my father, my origins—it had been so wrong of them not to tell me, so outrageously wrong—but the thought of becoming Keeper shot bolts of happiness through me. And Bertrand would love this news, I knew. I pictured us together, partners, overseers, protectors. We would be unsurpassable!

And as I ran to him, I realized he didn't even know that we were freeing the Bison today! So much had already happened this

day! I realized I hadn't seen him since he last flew over Helene and me, yesterday, before these many important revelations—before the ideas of mountains and ships and outrageous schemes of liberation.

I ran to Bertrand's nest and found it empty. Which was odd and unusual. I could not remember the last time I'd found his nest empty at night. He was a very regular sleeper, fond of his routine. But if he was not at home, I knew he would be at the waterfall, his favorite place. But when I arrived, he was not there. I went to the row of garbage cans near the plaza. He sometimes got hungry just before bedtime, so I raced there, expecting him to be feasting on fries or buns, but when I got there, I found no Bertrand. I did find Sonja and Angus, eating heartily from a bag of chips.

"Gotta keep our energy up," Angus explained.

"Of course," I said, and asked if either had seen Bertrand, and they said no, not since the afternoon, and though they were not particularly troubled by his absence, they agreed it would be good to locate him—if only to settle any last details for the liberation of the Bison—so we split up to look for him.

Angus said he'd look in the cathedral of flowers, where he'd known Bertrand to go occasionally, even at dusk, to take in the languid, lovely smell of night on leaves and petals. Sonja said she'd go toward the shore to see if any of the other gulls had seen

or heard from Bertrand—and if not, she could get them to aid in (and make quick work of) our search.

"I'm sorry I'm making a big deal out of this," I said, and they said not to worry, not to worry. Bertrand was needed, of course, and every moment was precious, given how close we were to beginning what I'd been thinking of as the Bison Freedom Gambit. So they rushed off, and I was happy they did not ask me where I would be looking, because I did not want to go, and did not want them to think the same terrible thought that was crawling on spindly spider legs into my consciousness.

When I arrived at the archery field, at first I saw nothing. Not a soul, not a remnant of human or mammal or bird. The wind was gusting, and the paper targets on the haybales were rippling, and I looked up at the sibling-suns with gratitude for this—this empty archery field.

But then I saw something white. It was on the ground, on the far end of the field. It was a small lump, a flash of something pale in the moonlight. Clothing, I thought. Some part of the humans' archery kits or clothes. I walked closer and saw gray, too—a gray half-circle that I decided could simply be the shadow under the human-clothing that was this shape.

Finally I drew closer and saw the yellow protuberance. A beak. His beak. It was Bertrand.

I stopped. Why go closer?

I wondered if I must get closer. Was it not enough to know he was gone? Why should I have to see him, his mangled body, the arrow piercing him—the fate he'd invited?

And I was angry. I was so angry with him. There was no reason for this, this senseless death. There was no reason to leave this world like this. To leave *me* like this! Selfish, I thought. Selfish, selfish, selfish.

How would I live with this? How will all of us who loved you, Bertrand, live with this? Forever we will see you on this field, we will think of your ignominious end. Why do this to us? Leave us with this? All for what?

All for what?

THIRTY-ONE

But then he stirred. Then he thrashed. A whirl of wings spun and flailed. I ran to him.

"You're alive!" I said.

"Oh," he said, finding me above him. "There you are," he said. He looked away. "I'm so ashamed."

The arrow had pierced his left wing.

"I've been trying to break it off," he said, "to shorten it, to be able to walk. I've been here since the late afternoon." Now his eyes were wet. Again he hid his face from me. "Oh, I'm so sorry. I'm so embarrassed. Oh, what stupidity!"

I wanted to agree that he should be embarrassed, and he was stupid, so profoundly stupid, but I am a practical animal and found myself focused on accomplishing the task at hand—breaking this arrow so he could right himself.

"Hold still," I said, and he did. He obeyed me from then on,

for which I was grateful. If I'd had to argue with him that night on the archery field I would not have made it through.

He held still, and I was about to jump on one end of the arrow when I heard the familiar sound of Angus sniffling through the grass. I waited, knowing that this would be far easier with his assistance.

"You see any sign of him?" Angus said as he approached. He could not see Bertrand yet, but when he did, he rushed to us.

"He's alive," he said to me. "You're alive," he said to Bertrand. "But what have you done?"

"I'm sorry," Bertrand said again, and we began strategizing on how to break or even extract the arrow, and in the middle of our deliberations, Sonja appeared, saying nothing. We could hear the solemn horror in her shallow breaths.

With the four of us on the task, we were able to first break the longer half of the arrow, the end containing the deadly silver point. Bertrand and I assumed that we would simply break the shorter end, too, leaving a length still lodged in Bertrand's wing, but it was Sonja who thought we could do more.

"Why not be rid of it?" she asked, and soon had her small jaws around the wooden arrow-shaft, and was pulling it away from Bertrand's wing. He grimaced and tears spilled from his eyes, but soon the arrow's bloody length came free and Sonja did what

I wanted to do, too—she ran with it in her mouth till she could hide it in a thicket where we would not have to see it, ever again.

"I'm so sorry," Bertrand said again.

He looked at each one of us, as if he planned to depart the world then and there, from the shame of it all.

"Stop that," Angus said. "You'll live."

"You will," I said, and Bertrand closed his eyes, releasing new tears. We all knew he would never fly the same again.

THIRTY-TWO

We had no time to linger, no time to recount how Bertrand had been felled. We needed to begin the liberation. Bertrand would have no place in it, given his recklessness, his silliness, but we would deal with all that another time.

We installed him in his nest, and we sutured his wound as well as we could. The others left, and I was leaving, too, when Bertrand beckoned me to stay.

"I'm so sorry, my friend," he said.

"Don't be sorry," I said.

"I was jealous," he said. "All that time you were spending with the goat. I guess I wanted to get your attention. Or impress you. None of it makes sense now. I'm so angry at my mind."

I hadn't known this, still can't believe this, that the mighty Bertrand would have been jealous of my time with Helene. Because time was short, I only said that it didn't matter, that he was my

greatest friend, that he was a paragon of valor.

"Valor, huh?" he said. "What I did was selfish and small. Just when every one of us is needed most, I'm out of commission. That's not valor."

"We will manage," I said.

"I'm so useless," he said.

"You are not useless," I said.

"I'm just a burden now," he said.

I told him he was not a burden, not at all, and I left him in his nest, knowing he would live and heal, but be forever earthbound. I worried about him, that whatever dark clouds were plaguing his mind would only grow when he missed this most heroic mission of ours.

Angus returned to the nest. His eyes were warm, sympathetic— but urgent, too.

"It's time," he said. "We have to begin."

I nuzzled Bertrand for a moment and then ran.

THIRTY-THREE

Angus and his time-machine were key to making all of this work, because the ship left at seven-oh-eight and only he and Helene had any idea what all these number-words meant. I knew just that we had to do it in the shortest amount of time, in order to maximize the chaos and minimize any possibility that any of the humans could figure out just what was happening in time to stop it all from happening.

This is what we were making happen:

It started with reconnaissance. Sonja and I had to figure out how many humans were minding the Bison that morning. Sometimes there were four. Sometimes only one. It was up to us to assess just how many humans we had to handle.

There was a light on at the Bison Enclosure Office, so Sonja jumped up to the windowsill and peeked in. She counted one

woman sitting at a desk, half-asleep with her feet up. Then there was the hammock-man, who roamed the perimeter, and this morning we found him—where else?—lying in his hammock strung between two tall pines.

We were thinking that this morning's humans were going to be particularly easy to handle when—no, no, no!—we saw a large vehicle pull up, its lights like white blades slicing through the woods, and four humans emerge.

They were the same humans who had been poking and prodding the Bison the day before. They were in uniform, with khaki pants and black jackets. They left the vehicle and made for the office with great confidence and determination. I looked up at Sonja with a look that said "Oh no." And she looked down at me with a look that said "I know."

But whether it was two humans or six, it was about to come down to Angus and Sharif and Johnson and the rest of the raccoons. The raccoons were hiding in a culvert when I came to them to report the human count. Angus was surprised but not daunted.

"So are we biting?" Sharif asked.

I hadn't heard anything about biting until that moment, and really didn't want to be part of any biting-of-humans. It never led anywhere good. Humans are deeply opposed to being bitten, and go to great lengths not to get bit, and they punish the biters

without mercy. I expressed my hesitance to Angus and his crew, who told me that my concerns were duly noted but that they would do what the situation required.

"We only bite for justice," Angus said, and I could not argue with that. Bite for justice. It had a certain ring.

Now Angus turned to his platoon of black and gray.

"We begin at six-twenty-one in the morning," he said. He turned to me. "That's just a few minutes from now."

It seemed that all of the raccoons could tell time now, and by my count, at least three of them had time-machines like Angus, were wearing them on their furry wrists, and could read them with casual confidence. I left them there, in the culvert, knowing that the next time I heard from them they would be inciting—we hoped—a lunatic bit of chaos in the parking lot.

Now I went to the Bison, who were, as planned, in the corner of the enclosure closest to the feeding station. The feeding station had a gate to the outside world—one the humans used to get into the feeding station. It was common for the Bison to gather there, in anticipation of being fed.

I skulked in the thicket nearby, and made a quick little yipping sound that we'd agreed would be my signal that all was a go.

Their return signal was to be a nod of the head, which they all did, almost in unison.

We were a go. I looked up to Yolanda, who was circling above, and gave her a nod. She let out a loud screech, signaling to everyone else that this thing was beginning.

And it began immediately.

It began when an alarm sounded from the black vehicle in which the official people had arrived. I looked over to find three raccoons on the vehicle's hood, scratching the paint, and Angus on top, urinating. The four uniformed humans, screaming and flailing, left the Bison office and ran to the car, which was making a deafening noise.

"Oh my god! Oh my god!" the humans from the office yelled as they ran to the car.

And now one door of the vehicle opened, and the human who got out also yelled "Oh my god! Oh my god!" and then quickly retreated back inside the vehicle.

Now the humans from the office were yelling "Oh my god! Oh my god!" as they circled the car, not really knowing what to do. The human was safe inside the car, and the office humans were safe at a certain distance, so it was funny for a long moment, watching the humans stand yelling "Oh my god! Oh my god!" while watching the raccoons do their scratching and thumping and urinating while these humans had no plan to stop it.

"Shoo!" roared one human.

And I laughed. I should not have laughed, because there was so much serious work to do, but I did laugh. The word *shoo* is such a funny one when applied to raccoons, because of all the animals under the Sun, the ones least likely to "shoo" are raccoons. They do not acknowledge the validity of the word.

Still, the humans said "Shoo, shoo," and even the raccoons stopped their scratching and urinating to laugh a bit, too.

But only for a second, because more distracting needed to be done. As the people approached with their *shoos* and waving arms, Angus and his friends jumped from the hood and the roof and began a madcap circling of the vehicle, running under it, jumping back onto the hood—anything to keep the humans in their khakis occupied. The one human who was still in the office came out, too, now on her phone. She was no doubt calling the Control-the-Animals people. We had anticipated this. Now it was time to cut the lights.

This was the work of the rats. They wanted to be involved some way in the liberation plan, and kept volunteering for various tasks, but we thought it best to limit them to this one key—crucial—task: to chew through the electrical wires such that when the chaos began, there would be no way to shed any light on it. And bless those rats, just as the madness around the vehicle was at its peak, the lights in the office and around the enclosure all went black. It was still a bit before dawn, so having this period of deepest darkness was essential.

And dark it was!

So, so dark. Wonderfully dark. We could see everything, of course, being animals and superior in the ways of sight, but we knew the humans would be utterly lost.

"We have a power outage," the office human said into her phone. "And the raccoons seem to be losing their minds."

Now I saw the other Bison-minder, the one who had been in the hammock before. He was walking slowly toward the office woman, slashing the darkness with his flashlight.

"What's happening?" he asked. Then his slashing light cut across me. "Ah! The coyote!" he yelled, and recoiled.

"Coyote?" the office human yelled, terror in her voice. "Where?"

Now that I was in the dark again, I have to admit that I was a bit scared, too—sure that the coyote must be near me, given the hammock-man had said the word immediately after slashing me with his light. I looked around, though, and saw nothing like a coyote. More importantly, I smelled no such creature. And I would have smelled anything new and unprecedented like a coyote a thousand miles away. It would have overwhelmed my nose.

And then I looked down and remembered.

"It's gone now," the man said. "But the raccoons are every-where. They've gone nuts!"

As he explained the raccoon-madness, I waited for the humans to move closer to the vehicle. The humans were still too close

to the Bison's feeding station. We needed the humans out of eyeshot.

Angus must have known this, too. He'd likely counted the humans who were gathered near the vehicle, and knew that two were missing. The raccoons' task was to distract all the humans, to draw them all away from the Bison enclosure.

But these two humans were hanging tight. He needed a more dramatic act.

"Ow! Oh god! One of 'em bit me!"

One of the khakied people had been bit, and I bet it was Angus who did it. He'd bitten for justice, and now this person was shrieking and jumping around, holding his ankle. And finally the two Bison-minders went out to the parking lot to help.

I am sorry that this biting happened.

It was not my idea.

There might have been other ways.

But in the moment, Angus acted, and the plan moved forward. With these final two gathered with the others around the still-alarming vehicle, and the one still inside it, trying to get the shrieking to end, the next stage of the plan could now begin.

With a triple-yip, I signaled Sonja to push the bolt of the enclosure door open. Though I could not see her from my vantage point, I could hear its distant tick as the metal moved left to right, and I knew that the door was ajar. I ran to the feeding

station, and saw that Freya and Samuel and Meredith were slowly and silently making their way out of the gate and into the open park. Oh wow.

Oh wow oh wow.

My friends, I can't tell you the vaulting joy I felt when I saw them pass through that gate! When I saw them drifting through—and then away from!—that metal grid of fencing, leaving that steel crosshatch behind! Oh wow it was something—far beyond what I imagined. My eyes watered, my throat dried, my heart darted everywhere in my body, from toe to toe and shoulder to shoulder, like a crazed dragonfly trying to escape.

But there was no time to dwell on this. It was Sonja's next job to lead the Bison away from the enclosure and into the woods and onto the beach, and it was my job to make sure that all went as planned with the horses.

Yes, the horses. We needed the horses. As haughty as they are, they were indispensable to this endeavor. With the Bison safely away, I ran to the horse stables and told them it was time. And they did their part with gusto. We had carefully selected three horses that were closest in size to Freya and Meredith and Samuel, and the horses' role now was to serve as stand-ins for the Bison. Moments after the Bison left, following Sonja into the woods, I led the horses into the enclosure, and to its farthest corner, away from the humans, so if they were to look across the field,

they would see three large lumps, Bison-like silhouettes, in the distance, huddled together and seemingly asleep. The horses, of course, would not pass for Bison upon close inspection, but at a glance, and to buy precious time, they would do. I watched them lope off across the field and settle in the corner, and I thought:

Well, that is not bad. Not at all bad.

As they settled into the corner, a siren rose in the distance. Ambulance, I thought. An ambulance for the person Angus bit. Good, I thought. A good distraction. And the person would be fine, for Angus had no diseases or ailments, not even bad breath—which is such a problem with so many of his kind.

Now it was time to catch up with Sonja and take her place in leading the Bison to the beach. I followed our agreed-upon route and with my speed I was soon upon their lumbering parade.

"Psst," I said to the rear of Samuel, who was in the rear.

"Psst yourself," he said to me, and I jogged quickly around him and to the head of the pack, to Sonja.

"How are we doing?" I asked.

"So far so good," she said. And she darted away, at a speed I found astonishing. I was always aware that she was quick—squirrels are quick, you know this, I trust—but I didn't know just how fast she was. She ran off in a straight line, to our left, and in seconds was a tiny dot. Then gone entirely. Gone! Surely she was not as fast as I, but still.

Still!

Her work from here on out was to circle the park, to assess any new people-movements, to gauge how effective our horse-decoys were, to fix any problems that needed fixing, and alert anyone who needed alerting.

With Sonja gone, and the smell of the ocean wafting through the trees, I turned to Freya.

"Are you ready?" I asked. "Soon we'll be at the windmill, and when we're at the windmill, we'll be among the goats, and when we're among the goats, it will be time to go."

"I know, my son. I know," she said, and chuckled. "Do you really think we'll make it? I'm far more nervous than I expected to be."

In the dim light I could just barely make out her eyes, and they did seem disquieted. Behind her, Meredith's breathing was quick, tense, on the verge of hyperventilating.

"Don't worry," I said. "Helene will take care of everything."

And just as I said it, I wondered if this were true. Helene was capable and bold, but could she really hide three enormous Bison among a herd of goats? We did not even know Helene very well. We were basing all this—so much!—on a goat we'd just met. That I'd just met, and whom the Bison didn't know at all! And hiding enormous Bison among relatively tiny goats? Oh, it was all such lunacy. We had not had time to test the theory. We had

not had time to worry or calculate or run through problems and solutions. We had only had time to guess at this idea and now we had to see it through.

THIRTY-FOUR

We emerged from the densest part of the forest and now we could see the windmill's silhouette, black against a sky of deepest blue.

"I smell the ocean," Freya said.

"Wait till you see it!" I said.

"I'm here," a breathless voice said.

"Helene?" I asked.

"Of course it's Helene," she said.

Now she emerged from the darkness and looked over my shoulder, up to the eyes of Freya.

"Ma'am," she said.

"Hello Helene," Freya said. "I am Freya, and this is Meredith, and this is Samuel."

"Hello, hello," Helene said, giving them each a quick bow.

And just then my chest ached, thinking in mere minutes I would have to say goodbye to Helene. She really was one of my favorite creatures—a thing of rare grace and radical kindness.

"Are you feeling ready?" she asked the Bison.

"I think so," Freya said, but she did not sound ready, and Meredith and Samuel said nothing. I could not see them well, but there was something new coming from them, some shaky pheromone, that told me they were tense at best and at worst, terrified.

"Follow me," Helene said, and we followed her down through the ice plants and toward what had been the field of tulips and then, from the tulips emerged a sea of goats. They had been sleeping, it seemed, and now they rose up, one by one, until we were surrounded by them, and they were already assessing whether or not they could do what they had been asked to do—to surround and hide these mighty Bison.

"Helene, this is crazy," one said. "Look at me."

This goat, whose name was Theo, stood next to Freya, showing just how tiny he was in her shadow.

"She's huge!" he said, then looked up to Freya. "No offense."

The sky was beginning to shed its night cloak.

"None taken," Freya said, and I could see in her eyes an exhausted sadness. Meredith and Samuel were looking around them, at the goats converging from all sides, and though they smiled

politely, they did not seem to be embracing the moment. Did not seem to believe the plan could work.

And for a moment, Helene faltered, too. I saw something in her eyes, something uncertain. Something like fear.

"Today..." I whispered to her.

She lifted her chin. "Today," she said to the goats assembled.

"Today we do something important," I whispered, and she glanced at me. Now her eyes were bright and sure.

"Today we do something new, something important, and something very risky," she roared in a bell-clear voice.

Everyone around—the goats, the Bison, me—was instantly locked into attention.

"It will take total commitment, total belief," she said, louder now. It was as if she had taken the wind from the ocean, had eaten the clouds from the sky. "It will take everything we have."

I was so moved by her commanding tone, by her utter resolve, that I found myself wanting for it all to begin immediately.

"Now we *act*," she said, and I tapped my paw on the ground, in a way I hoped she would read as gently impatient. What if the escape of the Bison was hampered by someone making endless speeches about the escape of the Bison? How long would we wait to begin?

Not long. Just then, far away, a whistle sounded. It was a human whistle, the kind made when they put their fingers in

their mouths. It is an impressive trick—one very few humans can do on their own, with their own flesh, without their machines.

"That's the goatherd," Helene said.

Until that point, I hadn't heard of any goatherd. But now, in the faraway distance, I could see a man in a wide-rimmed black hat. It was the human who had been with them the first day.

"That's the goatherd," I said.

"Indeed," Helene said. "Now, the first group knows what to do. Go now." And at her command, a group of twelve goats ran off toward the goatherd, and when they came upon him, they sprinted past him, and toward the jagged boulder that separated us from the port. The plan was these goats would rush toward the ship, forcing the goatherd to rush with them, chasing them, desperate to get ahead. He would not allow them to reach the ship before him, so this would keep him occupied and out of the way. Of this Helene was sure.

"He'll be very surprised," Helene noted. "Never before have any of us rushed to get back *on* that boat."

And so we watched the goats run up the hill, and watched the goatherd—I love this word, *goatherd*—run after them. Which left a hundred or so goats still back near the windmill, ready and waiting to do the principal work of the escape, which was to cloak the Bison in goat-chaos.

This was everything, really. The heart of the plan. The part that had to work, lest all else be in vain.

"Ready?" Helene asked the Bison.

A long pause—a terribly long pause—ensued. None of the Bison said anything. But finally Freya nodded.

"Yes," she said, and Meredith and Samuel nodded, too, though they seemed less certain than Freya.

"Go!" Helene roared, and the goats converged upon the Bison, forming a tight mass, jumping and swirling, baying and zigzagging. The hope was to create a mass of manic activity such that if the goatherd looked back at all, he would only see a thrashing forest of goats, moving steadily toward the ship. And in the dim light, we hoped, the goatherd would not see the three enormous Bison hidden in this moving goat-forest.

Besides, it was not so far. The mass of goat and Bison only had to get over the dunes, then onto the flat stretch of beach—a distance I could travel in seconds—and then up the promontory and finally down to the ship.

And now we were moving.

We were quickly in the dunes, and between the dark and the distraction of the goatherd, all was good. We were simply an inland wave of fur and hair and legs. No one could tell a Bison from a dog from a goat in that light, among those dunes.

We were moving steadily, the Bison trudging among the frantic goats, keeping their heads low, and I was circling, weaving in and out of the mass, assessing how it looked from outside—good, good, fine, better than expected!—while also periodically reassuring Bison and goats alike that all was working, that all we had to do was continue.

When we made it down the oceanward side of the dunes, and saw the long stretch of flat beach before us, I laughed a bit, knowing we were on our way, and there was not all that much left to do.

"It's so far!" Meredith said.

"I was just thinking about the distance," I told Meredith, "and I was thinking it's *not* so far."

Now Freya seemed unsure. "It really is a greater distance than I anticipated," she said. "And that boulder! It's high and so rocky."

This trepidation in her voice! It was hard for me to hear.

"We need to go faster," Helene said.

This was confirmed seconds later, when a heavy thump of wings filled the air. I knew it was Yolanda.

"Time's short!" she yelled. "Time's short!"

She explained that the raccoons had only been able to hold off the khakied humans for a short while after we had left. Apparently

some new humans came with lights and nets and darts and the threat of guns—and the raccoons had understandably cleared out. The humans had then entered the Bison enclosure, suspicious about the Bison being Bison.

"In the light, the horses did not look so much like Bison," Yolanda explained. "So as soon as the humans came near, the horses bolted. They bolted and jumped and went nuts."

"As a means of distraction, I hope," I said.

"Yes, yes! Of course!" Yolanda said.

The horses had run around the enclosure, kicking and rearing and scaring the humans, and finally they'd escaped entirely—jumping the fence that the Bison never could. The horses cleared it like it was nothing.

"You should have seen it!" Yolanda said. "Then they scattered all over the park." She thought, and I agreed, that it was both advantage and problem: the horses would occupy the Parks People, who would have to track the horses down and bring them back to the stables. But at the same time, so much action in the park in general would likely bring more people, more Control-the-Animals people and maybe even Parks Police. This would not be good for our quiet pre-dawn escape.

"So you better get moving," Yolanda said. "Oh, and Angus said you only have eighteen minutes. Whatever that means."

I didn't know what that meant, but I looked to Helene and she confirmed that we needed to move. We had to get the Bison into the belly of the ship without anyone noticing. Only if no one suspected anything odd would the ship be allowed to leave on schedule. Even if everyone in the park knew the Bison were missing—and surely they knew by now—no one could know that they'd gone to the ship.

So we only had to get them aboard unseen.

"We'll be a thousand miles across the sea before anyone would guess," Helene said. "Far too late to turn back."

THIRTY-FIVE

There was a short amount of time, and a short distance for the Bison to cover still, and I had a key task to perform to keep everything going—to signal the start of the final stage of the escape. So I ran to the top of the hill that separated all that the Bison would be leaving behind from the ship that would take them to their future, their liberation. It was my job to run to the top, and make sure all was ready for the last steps of the journey.

I flew up the hill, which was rocky and volcanic and hurt my paws briefly and inconsequentially, and then I was there, at the top, and I could see it all. The long stretch of the beach where the goats and Bison were rumbling toward the hill and me, and, on the other side of the peak, the ship. The ship!

I had not seen the ship before this. I had seen ships, yes. I had often seen them from far away, on the sea, and had occasionally

seen them pass closer to our shore, but had never seen one stopped like this, so close, right there!

And it was right there!

And it was enormous!

It was as big as any building in the park, and brighter, lit by a million lights of white and blue and yellow.

It looked very beautiful to me, and very strange, and very man-made, and also like a constellation of low-hanging sister suns. I knew I would freeze from the beauty if I did not look away, so I looked away, at the horizon where the sky meets the sea, and that's when I saw the first crack of orange. The first break in the black of night. The Sun was coming.

Now time was short. So short.

I made my signal, which was the loudest howl I could howl, which was also my favorite thing to say:

Ha ha hooooo!

I yelled it from the top of that black mini-mountain.

Ha ha hooooo!

I yelled it to the beach and I yelled it to the ship and I yelled it to the sky. Especially to the sky, because it was the birds who needed most to hear my signal-song.

Ha ha hooooo!

Helene had explained that the ship held few humans, fewer than ten, and the attention of these humans had to be diverted so that

when the mass of goat and Bison descended the hill and rumbled up the ramp and into the boat, few or no humans would be there to see it.

Ha ha hoooooo!

I roared again, and from above I heard Yolanda say, "Got it. We're on it. We're going," as she swooped over me and toward the ship. But it was not just her. No.

She was joined by five, ten, a billion other birds. Not just pelicans and gulls, but also loons, and also herons, and sandpipers, and even blue jays and hummingbirds and crows! It was a tremendous sight, all these birds in their different colors and different ways of flying, all in a swarm heading toward the great ship, with madness on their minds.

They quickly swooped to the far side of the ship, the side opposite the ramp. The idea was to keep the ship's humans occupied on that side, fending off the bird onslaught, for long enough that the Bison could get down the hill and into the ship without any of these humans noticing.

Oh this was a big part of the plan.

A risky and crazy and unavoidable part of the plan.

And the part of the plan I thought most likely to fail.

But I watched and it did not fail.

No. It did not fail. It was glorious.

The birds swarmed on the far side of the ship, and first there were yells. I could hear the human yells, even from so far away!

Then there were plumes of water. Somehow the humans on the ship could direct plumes of water upward, like the fountain near the cathedral of flowers, and I saw these white sprays of water go up, I watched as my bird friends simply rose up to miss them. It was so easy. Birds can move up, I wanted to tell the plume-wielding humans. You send the water up, the birds just go farther up!

Oh it was something!

Oh humans. Bless them, they try.

And it seemed that it was all of the humans on the ship who were trying. I am not a good counter, as you know, but it seemed that ten, twelve, or more of the humans were all gathered on the far side of the ship, yelling and pluming and ducking when the occasional Yolanda or crow swung out of the sky to send them scurrying. It was working. I looked and looked with my extraordinary vision and saw no humans on the near side of the ship.

It was time.

I made a second signal, this one to bring the goats and Bison up to the top of the hill for our last push, and when I made this signal—ha ha hooooohoooo!—I did so with such joy. I was laughing at the end of the signal, so overcome with happiness was I, picturing the last thundering stage of the gambit, because I knew it would work. Everything was working, everything was

beautiful, and now they had heard my signal-song and were climbing the hill.

And oh!

Oh oh oh, it was something to see. Everything I'd ever seen till then was dull and uninspired compared with the way those goats went up the hill with the Bison between them.

I should have known!

Of course the goats' work now would be bigger, crazier, better, heightened. We were drawing closer to the ship, where humans would be, and closer to the goatherd, who might see, and thus more hiding of the Bison needed to be done, and to that end, the goats ran, and jumped, and scurried, and climbed on each other's back, in such a way that it looked like a big rolling ball of fur and ears and horns, lopsided and crazed. And they were rolling *up* hill! Even though I knew that Freya and Meredith and Samuel were among the goats, *I could not see them.* I knew they were there but even I could not see them!

The goats were *that good*!

And Helene was especially good. I could see her leading it all. Jumping, circling, commanding. "Higher!" she said. "Loonier!" she said. And occasionally she reminded the Bison to stay low, to hide their horns, to keep themselves unseeable.

And then they were there with me.

It happened so fast. I was watching the mass of goats and Bison at the base of the hill, and seconds later, it seemed, they were with me, at the top. They were heaving. They were exhausted. They could not speak, could not even look up. Freya was on her knees. Meredith and Samuel lay down on the volcanic peak—not a comfortable place to lie, I was sure. I had not expected the climb to take so much out of them, but then again, I had never seen them run more than a few feet at a time, so I could only smile, and wait, and while allowing them to recover, my heart filled with an electric bliss, seeing them so high above the park and sand and sea. From where we were, we could see the windmill, and the taller buildings of the park, and the humans' cement corridors around it, and could see the sweep of sand and dunes and sea. We could see everything we'd ever seen, and a thousand times more.

"You made it," I said. I tried to say.

"Don't cry," Freya said, her voice so weak. I was not yet crying, but my throat was hitching my speech, and between their heavy breathing from the climb up the hill, and my sniffling and snorting, we all took a second to gather ourselves. And while we did so, the crack in the horizon opened up like a curtain raised to a spectacular array of color and light.

"Oh! Oh!" Samuel said, rising. He looked to the Sun and sea. "It's beyond anything I could have imagined."

And it was then that I realized that during all their running and being hidden on the beach, they had not yet seen the ocean.

"Oh," Meredith sighed. "Just look at it."

"See the pinks, and lavenders, and chartreuse and silver," Samuel said. "I see gold! Look at all the gold! The sea is gold!"

I don't think I'd ever heard him so happy. His eyes were fully open for the first time.

"I'm so grateful you brought us here," Freya said to me and to Helene. "I never thought I'd see it."

"Oh, you'll see plenty more of it," Helene said. "You'll be on the sea for weeks. You might see more of it than you want to, honestly. Every day and night until you get to the main-land."

Then Freya turned to me. I will always remember her eyes at that moment. There was pity in them, and apology, and a bit of frustration—as if she were mad at me for making her say something she thought so obvious.

"We can't," she said.

"Can't what?" I asked.

"We can't go on that ship," she said.

"But it's right down there," I said. "We've already done the hard part. Everything's ready." I was frantic, for the sky was growing brighter, and with every passing moment it would be more difficult to hide them as they descended the hill.

"No," Freya said. "We're not going. We thought perhaps we could, but this journey, short as it has been, has proven we are not ready for more. We can't make it."

"You can!" I wailed.

"It's impossible," she said.

These words! I couldn't speak. They were such madness, these words. A betrayal! After all this toil, all this planning! I looked to Samuel, whose head was hung low. I looked to Meredith, who smiled grimly at me.

"We had our doubts all along," she said. "Honestly, we never thought any of this would work."

Samuel looked up. "We didn't think we'd get this far."

"But why let me—let all of us—go through all this trouble?" I asked. And now I saw that Helene, and all the goats, had heard our conversation, and they shared my irritation. They were leaning in, curious but with growing exasperation.

"You needn't be angry," Freya said. "Or sad. Or even surprised. Look at us. We're not adventurers. We're lumbering old mammals. We were not meant to shoot across the sea in strange boats."

"I'm sorry, kid," Samuel said.

"Seeing this is enough," Freya said. She was still staring at the phosphorescent sea, which had grown brighter, whiter, the waves topped with frosting. She turned to me then. "Thank you, my

son." She turned to Helene and the goats. "You all have given us a precious thing. We are so grateful."

With a flurry of wings Yolanda was among us.

"What's happening?" she asked. "We're running out of tricks over there at the ship."

"They're not going," I said.

Yolanda looked to the Bison, incredulous, shattered.

And finally Freya, who had disappointed me so much in all this, with her decision and her few words of explanation, raised her voice to speak to us all.

"We have lived cloistered lives. Limited lives. But you have freed our eyes and our minds. What you did today mattered. It did. It mattered a great deal. You gave us the sea. You gave us this unbounded sight. And we will not forget it."

"But you have to go!" I said.

"No, no," Freya said. "All along we wondered if we wanted to board a boat with both destination and fate unknown. We are not young. We are not fast. And even getting this far has taxed our every muscle and every bone. We've been in the park all our lives, and what remains of our lives is finite. We don't want to die in some unknown place, so far from home. And die we would. We hope you will take pride in what you did today, and will accept our gratitude."

She swept her eyes across the mass of goats before her.

"You have done a brave and kind thing for us today," she said. "And we will never be able to thank you properly—"

A whistle cut her speech short. It was the same one from before, a human whistle. It was the goatherd. He was standing on the ramp to the boat, looking up. He no doubt could see the goats amassed at the top of the hill, and no doubt wondered why they were there. He whistled again.

"Goodbye," Helene said to Freya and Samuel and Meredith, and very quickly the Bison said their goodbyes to all the goats who had run and jumped and bayed to keep them hidden all this time. There was much confusion and some frustration, but there was also a sense of urgency, for the boat was leaving.

"Go on," Helene said to her goat army, and they began to make their way down the hill, toward the ramp and the goatherd, and as they passed me and Yolanda and Sonja, they all said good-bye to us with baying and occasional licking and a few tears, too. This was new. I'd never seen a goat cry, let alone a thousand of them sobbing at once.

I was overcome. I was jittery. I blinked through tears and tried to organize my mind. Was all this for naught? And would we all simply go back to the park? What would await us there? I thought of the Parks Police, and the Control-the-Animals people, how they had been pursuing me already—and how much closer they would be paying attention after this failed escape. I stood on the peak of

that small mountain as the Sun awakened the world, and did not know what to do.

Then Helene said this:

"You could come with us."

THIRTY-SIX

I had just thought the same thought. That I could go.

That I could go.

That I could go.

I could go.

I could go. I

could go. I could go.

And that perhaps I was meant to go.

"You could run as much as you like," Helene said.

And this was true. By her telling, there would be all the land I could ever want—I could run for a million days and never find a boundary.

"And those rectangles you like?" she said. "Those are actually pictures of the mainland. I didn't know when to tell you. They're pictures of all the places and things on the mainland, and some of them are just imaginings of things that could happen there, or anywhere. There are millions of things like that, inside rectangles and outside rectangles—more than you could ever see or want to see.

"And there are free dogs," she said. "A million free dogs."

"And coyotes?" I said.

"A billion of those!" Helene said, laughing. "You could run with them and see. Because there is so, so much to see. And if you are truly the Eyes, truly alive to see and run, I think you should come."

Every word she said was such simple truth. Such clarity. Such inevitability. And I knew that I *could* easily slip onto the ship. That would be nothing. And I *could* easily remain among the goats, hidden and respected and aided whenever needed.

"We will protect you," Helene said. "And when you get to the mainland, you can stay with us, or simply run free. You can run free for a thousand years."

I thought about this.

I knew it was true.

I knew I would go.

And I knew I needed to see Bertrand.

THIRTY-SEVEN

Helene understood completely. And because we no longer had to sneak three enormous mammal-mountains on the ship, every-thing was now looser, easier. I had time to find my friend.

"Just be quick. We have only a few minutes," Helene said.

And I laughed. I laughed as I flew down the hill and across the beach and made a spectacular diagonal across the park. Just be quick! Just be quick, she said! I laughed and laughed until I encountered Angus, red-eyed, coming from the direction of Bertrand's nest.

"He's not there," he said, his voice cracking.

"Where is he?" I asked.

Now Angus was blubbering. He could barely form words.

"He's flying his last flight. Look behind you. Over the sea."

And though I did not want to, I turned around and looked up. And there, high in the white sky, I saw a tiny jagged shape. It

was Bertrand, flying over the ocean, flying crookedly, desperately in his final flight.

No! I thought. Not the coda. Not now.

"You go," Angus said. "I'll catch up."

And I ran.

I ran to the ocean faster than I'd ever run before. And now that I knew I was half-coyote, and that my coyote blood gave me my speed, and perhaps my eyes, too, I embraced it all and ran with the power of all dogs, all coyotes, every one of them who had come before me.

"Bertrand!" I yelled as I ran, but I was still far away, and the spiraling bird in the sky kept climbing. Please stop, I prayed. Please hear me, I prayed. I looked to the Sun and asked for her help. Please, please, I huffed as I ran.

And soon I could see the ocean, its froth and wind, and I saw Bertrand more clearly now. I could see him high above, flying a thousand feet in the sky, directly above the hill where Helene and Sonja and Yolanda still stood.

Oh Bertrand, I thought. No. Please don't.

I ran to the rock. I thought if I got to the top of the rock I could roar to him, I could howl to him and ask him to stop. I could tell him he didn't have to do this.

I knew that this was the kind of drama, kind of theater, that he loved so much. He would see this as heroic.

I raced to the beach and there I saw the usual line of gulls on the shore, watching Bertrand in their usual solemn manner. A few of them glanced at me as I passed, closing their eyes to me in acknowledgment of my friendship with Bertrand, who would soon be dead in this most honorable way.

I flew across the beach and instantly I was upon the rock and scaled it in three bounds and at its peak I joined Helene and Yolanda and Sonja. They were watching with tears soaking their feathers and fur. "Oh Johannes, I can't look," Helene said. "Is this really something you all do here? It's awful."

"Bertrand!" I yelled to the sky.

"It's no use," Yolanda said. "It's custom. You know this is their idea of honor. We can't change it."

"Bertrand!" I roared again to the sky.

The crooked-flying bird that was Bertrand made no indication he had heard. He was rising higher and higher and higher, and this meant he would soon let go. This was what the end-end was like—a theatrical flying in ever-rising gyres until finally the gull lets go, they cease their fighting to stay aloft, and they fall. Finally they fall, fall, fall, until they crash to the sea and are gone.

"Bertrand!" I howled again, and this time Bertrand's faraway silhouette seemed to falter. "Come down here!" I yelled.

But the faltering was just prelude to falling. The magnificent bird that was Bertrand began to drop from the sky.

"Stop!" I yelled.

He plummeted like a ragged mess of bone and feather.

"Please!" I roared.

I summoned the earth. I summoned the clouds. I summoned the Sun. "Bertrand," I yelled. "There is more!"

THIRTY-EIGHT

Just before he struck the hard line of the sea, he spread his wings, stopped his downward fall, and managed, in his depleted state, to steady himself. Then, with a few more uncertain flaps, he rose and grew stronger. In seconds he had flown all the way to us, and landed on our high rock. He seemed very put out.

"What were you yelling about?" he asked. "I was in the middle of something."

"I noticed," I said.

He straightened himself out and tried to look dignified and even casual, even though he was a bit of a mess.

"Okay, what is it?" he asked.

"How about," I said, "you don't die? Come with me."

"Where? Back to the park? You know I can't. A bird of my species has his pride, you know. We have our customs. I can't—"

"No," I said. "Leave. Go over the ocean, with me. On this ship. The Bison aren't going, but we can."

Helene was standing next to me, and she nodded, though she had not envisioned this scenario, where both a coyote-dog and a broken-down gull would be joining them. But how hard could it be?

"You have more to see and do," I said to Bertrand.

"Go with you? On that?" he asked, nodding to the ship. The idea of not dying, of instead coming with me, was a distant thing to him, but it was growing closer. I could tell its contours and shape were becoming clear to him.

"You're not old," I said. "You're only changed. Before, you could fly, and now, you can walk. Hold on to me as we run together and see. See the sea, see the main-land. See everything that can be seen."

"So I'd ride on your back?" he asked.

"Sometimes," I said. "And sometimes you can walk."

An impish smile overtook him. "That would be pretty slow," he said, and I laughed.

"To be honest, I wasn't so crazy about dying," he said. "I mean, I was going to make it look spectacular and all."

"Of course," I said.

"But I was also thinking it would be pretty good *not* to die."

"So come," I said.

"When?" he asked.

"Now," Helene said. "We have to go now."

There were about ten goats left near us, and Helene urged us to sneak in among them as they made their way down the hill.

"Stand on my back," I told Bertrand, and he did. He weighed so little! All this time, for a thousand years, he'd flown merrily above me, and all this time I hadn't known how light he was. I could have been carrying him all this time!

"This doesn't mean I'm going," he said. "I'm just thinking on your way to the ship."

Hiding a dog and a bird was no great feat for the goats. We were so much smaller than the Bison, so we made our way down the hill without any fear of detection. And soon we were at the bottom of the hill, where the land met the dock, and were approaching—fast—the ramp to the ship.

"What will we eat?" Bertrand asked.

I laughed, and he laughed, because we both knew that anything we usually ate would be in infinite supply where we were going. It was such a silly question.

"Will we ever come back to this place?" he asked, and though I assumed the answer was no, Helene surprised us both.

"Maybe," she said. "Who knows? We got here once. Maybe we get here again."

We looked up the hill, and I hoped to see the Bison again, to tell them what we were doing, but they were gone—they'd disappeared down the other side of the boulder. The only one of my friends still on the peak was Sonja. She waved. She was grinning, waving, crying, so many things all at once, and now she would be the Eyes. That was obvious to me and to her and would be obvious to all. The Eye? Is that what they'd call her, given she only had the one? I laughed for it was so fitting and right. I was happier for her than I'd ever felt for myself. She would be so good.

And soon the herd was herding us up the metallic incline, and Bertrand and I were among them, and I felt the steel under my paws, and felt the tension of a ramp over water, and then we were inside. Inside the belly of the ship.

The smell was strong. The light was gone.

"We did it," Helene said.

LAST CHAPTER

Helene told us to sleep and we slept. With all the planning and escaping, I had not slept in ages. We slept among a thousand goats in a cramped dark space, the smell outrageous, but when I woke, I saw that Bertrand was just waking, too, and he smiled at me, and I smiled, too.

"What in God's name are we doing?" he asked.

I didn't know what to say. I couldn't believe we had done what we did. I was sure that we were already a million miles from the park, from all that we'd ever known. There was one small window in the hold, and I squeezed my way through the goats to this porthole, dusted with sea salt, and saw only blue—blue sky, blue water without end.

"I really thought I'd be dead," Bertrand said when I returned to him. "Now I'm on a ship among goats. And they smell so bad!"

I shushed him, not wanting to offend our hosts, who were sleeping all around us.

"You didn't have to die," I said to him.

"And you didn't have to stay there," he said to me. "All this time, you thought you needed to stay in the park, but then you left. And now you're here, and soon we'll be somewhere else."

When he said that, I panicked, ever so briefly. I thought about all I loved in the home we'd left. Our friends there. Freya, Meredith, Samuel. The trees, the flowers, the children, the music. And for a moment I wanted to leap. To jump and swim home.

But I couldn't. I knew this. You know this.

What kind of coyote-dog would I be if I were not out in the world running? What kind of Eyes would I be if I were not out in the world seeing?

Heroes go forth.

To be alive is to go forth.

So we went forth.

A NOTE ABOUT THE ART

The paintings in this book are classical landscapes by artists long departed.
Shawn Harris, the frequent collaborator of this book's author, added Johannes to each landscape
but otherwise left the paintings as they were.

pp. 8-9 Paul Joseph Constantin Gabriël, *Landscape near Abcoude*, 1860–1870
Rijksmuseum, Amsterdam, The Netherlands

pp. 38-39 Jacob van Ruisdael, *The Forest Stream*, ca.1660
The Metropolitan Museum of Art, New York, NY

pp. 64-65 Berndt Lindholm, *Forest Interior*, 1878
Finnish National Gallery, Helsinki, Finland

pp. 100-101 Narcisse-Virgile Diaz de la Peña, *In the Forest*, 1874
National Gallery of Art, Washington, D.C.

pp. 128-129 Gustave Courbet, *La Bretonnerie in the Department of Indre*, 1856
National Gallery of Art, Washington, D.C.

pp. 158-159 Fanny Churberg, *Inside the Forest*, 1871–1872
Finnish National Gallery, Helsinki, Finland

pp. 192-193 André Giroux, *Forest Interior with a Waterfall, Papigno*, 1825–1830
National Gallery of Art, Washington, D.C.

pp. 222-223 Ferdinand von Wright, *Forest Landscape from Haminalahti*, 1880
Finnish National Gallery, Helsinki, Finland

pp. 250-251 William Trost Richards, *Quiet Seascape*, 1883
Minneapolis Institute of Art, Minneapolis, MN

COVER & ENDPAPERS

IN THE MCSWEENEY'S EDITION: Paul Joseph Constantin Gabriël, *Landscape near Abcoude*, 1860–1870
Rijksmuseum, Amsterdam, The Netherlands

IN THE KNOPF EDITION: Berndt Lindholm, *Forest Interior*, 1878
Finnish National Gallery, Helsinki, Finland

ACKNOWLEDGMENTS

Thank you to these invaluable early readers: Em-J Staples, Sarah Stewart Taylor, Heather Rader and her students, and of course VV, BV, and AV. Thank you to Shawn Harris, Justin Carder, Claire Astrow, Caroline Sun, and Sunra Thompson. This book would be nowhere without its tireless champions: Amanda Uhle, Amy Sumerton, Melanie Nolan, Andrew Wylie, Luke Ingram, and the editor of editors, Taylor Norman.

Thank you also to members of the Young Editors Project (www.youngeditorsproject.org), which allows young readers to see books in manuscript form, and become part of the publishing process. Students who lent me their time and expertise include: Sandra Jobson-Aue of Berkeley, California; Vi and Abe DePasquale, and Clara Herbert of Ann Arbor; Alba Villacis, Callahan Damon, Cheehan Ma, Elena Popov, and Kailey Gallagher from Northfield, Illinois; Cara Sanderson from Doncaster, England; Corinne Licardo from New York, New York; Elena Garcia Sheridan from Wollongong, Australia; Emmett Jackson from Fayetteville, Arkansas; Henry Martin from Elsah, Illinois; Noah Dimond from Yorkshire, England; Orla Tangeman from Southport, England; Sydnee Faria from Richmond, British Columbia; and the following sharp minds from Ottawa, Ontario: Catherine, Penelope, Emma, Ismail, Mia, Ana, Naila, Lillian, Jennifer, Jackson, Theo, Katherine, Haadyah, Luca, Christopher, Madilyn, Norah, Caryss, Nicolas, Marlon, Richard, Henry, Chris, Kate, Kaedence, Santiago, Mateaus, Ajim, Tina, Adnan, Asher, Cameron, Aaron, Lexi, Jayden, Anthony, Oscar, Zara, Ana, Ahmed, Will, Tilly, Amelia, Alex, Emma, Ramona, Theo, Olivia, Koki, Avery, and Arya.

ABOUT THE AUTHOR

Dave Eggers is the author of many books, including *The Every*, *The Circle*, *The Monk of Mokha*, and the National Book Award finalist *A Hologram for the King*, as well as numerous books for young readers, including *Her Right Foot*, *Faraway Things*, and *The Lifters*. He is the founder of the independent publishing company McSweeney's and the college-access nonprofit ScholarMatch, and the co-founder of 826 Valencia, a youth writing center that has inspired dozens of other centers worldwide. He is the winner of the Muhammad Ali Humanitarian Award for Education and the Dayton Literary Peace Prize.